# BAD GIRLS
# IN LOVE

# BAD GIRLS IN LOVE

## CYNTHIA VOIGT

*AN ANNE SCHWARTZ BOOK*
ATHENEUM BOOKS FOR YOUNG READERS
New York   London   Toronto   Sydney   Singapore

For Merrilee,
who knows about love—

And for Emily and Morgan,
too (be they good or be they bad, on any given day)—

And also for Brian,
who appreciates all three of them on all given days

Atheneum Books for Young Readers
An imprint of Simon & Schuster Children's Publishing Division
1230 Avenue of the Americas, New York, New York 10020

Book design by Ann Sullivan
The text for this book is set in Janson Text.

Printed in the United States of America
2 4 6 8 10 9 7 5 3 1

Library of Congress Cataloging-in-Publication Data
Voigt, Cynthia.
Bad girls in love / by Cynthia Voigt.
p. cm.
"An Anne Schwartz book."
Summary: Now in the eighth grade, best friends Mikey and Margolo try to
figure out boys, crushes, and falling in love.
ISBN 0-689-82471-8
[1. Interpersonal relations—Fiction. 2. Friendship—Fiction. 3. Schools—
Fiction.] I. Title.

PZ7.V874 Baf 2002
[Fic]-dc21
2001045898

FIRST
EDITION

# CONTENTS

# WEEK ONE

## GIRL MEETS BOY

# 1
# THE CALM BEFORE THE STORM

T hey're probably going to announce who got what part."

Mikey spoke against background cafeteria sounds of talk and laughter, clattering dishes, and scraping chairs.

"In assembly," she said. "In . . ." she looked at her watch, compared it with the clock on the wall, "twenty minutes, or maybe fifteen. Are you nervous?"

Mikey Elsinger and Margalo Epps claimed to have been best friends since the first day of fifth grade, which wasn't exactly true. It could have been if they had been willing to modify their claim with an *almost*—best friends since *almost* the first day—but neither one of them wanted to be modified, or to be a modifier, either.

"Why *did* you try out for the play, anyway?" Mikey asked. Margalo wasn't the kind of person who tried to get people to notice her by putting herself up on a stage, or out on a tennis court. What had gotten into her?

Margalo said, "It's Jennet Jourdemayne," which explained nothing to anybody other than herself, but Margalo didn't intend anybody to learn her secret reason, not even Mikey. Especially since Mikey was the last person who'd sympathize.

"It's because I told you last year you were a good actress."

Margalo welcomed the wrong guess. It was bad enough having this horrible hopeless crush on a teacher, but it would be ten times worse if anybody found out about it. And what if he found out about how she felt? Margalo's whole body blushed hot at that thought. It wasn't as if she didn't know that no healthy-minded grown-up man would want a fourteen-year-old girlfriend, even if he wasn't already married. She knew that. But she still hoped, and she couldn't believe how stupid that was. But as long as nobody knew—absolutely nobody, not even Aurora—and Margalo trusted her mother, but she still wasn't going to tell her—because as long as she was the only one who knew, she was safe.

So Margalo didn't tell Mikey that her guess was way off. But neither did she say it was right on. Instead, she looked mysterious, with a little smile that almost admitted it matched by eyebrows that absolutely denied it. In fact, Margalo was enjoying herself. Even if the secret you know is about yourself—and mostly just makes you miserable—still, knowing something nobody else even suspects will increase your self-confidence. Secrets are like that. Besides, it isn't every day you can use the same facial expression to irritate somebody twice.

Mikey knew this trick of Margalo's. She took a gloppy spoonful of chocolate pudding into her mouth, closed her lips firmly, and stared back at her friend while she pushed pudding out between her teeth, then sucked it back onto her tongue, then swallowed it.

Margalo counterpunched. She peeled back the skin on her banana, peeling it down carefully, strip by strip, taking each strip no more than a third of the way down at each peeling, carefully rotating the banana as she carefully, methodically, peeled it.

They played out their two-man scene to their audience of two until Mikey got bored, and broke eye contact, and groused, "Next thing, you'll be going to the dance. With a date."

Margalo knew better. "I'm not even invited to parties."

"Yeah, but neither am I, and I'm a good athlete." Then Mikey wondered, "We don't *want* to be invited to their parties, do we? Do you? I don't. The stuff that goes on—"

"Definitely squalid," Margalo agreed.

Mikey and Margalo tended to agree about things. Their quarrels were mostly for style, not substance. They had them because otherwise life would be too tedious, and discouraging. From the start junior high had been bad, and this year it had only gotten worse. In eighth grade school seemed to be all about couples and love and/or sex and/or everything-in-between.

Everything-in-between covered a lot of territory. There

5

were *crushes*, for one, or a girl would *have a thing about* a boy. Boys *liked* girls. Boys and girls *really liked* one another, or *really cared for, really cared about* one another. But was it love?

Mikey and Margalo had discussed it—of course. Their level of accomplishment in love-and-sex-and-everything-in-between was the same: Never been on a date, never been kissed. It was their attitudes that differed. Mikey was mostly outraged—*What's the big deal? Who cares?* Whereas Margalo projected scientific detachment—*Aren't human beings bizarre creatures?* They had their different attitudes and they each liked having the differing attitudes they had, while at the same time they both agreed that nobody understood either sex or love. But wasn't it curious, as Margalo pointed out, that there was a sex-ed unit in gym, but no love-ed unit in any other class?

They also agreed that they didn't plan to be kept ignorant. As Mikey pointed out, ignorance isn't bliss, it's not knowing something. Not knowing something always put you at a disadvantage, in Mikey's opinion, and that was not where she cared to be.

But it wasn't easy to find out anything about sex, or love, or everything-in-between, especially if you weren't invited to parties. That meant you had to get your field information from secondary sources, and it was Margalo's opinion that people often avoided telling the truth, especially the whole truth and nothing but, about those subjects.

As far as they could tell, the parties seemed to be about slow dancing, close dancing, and long bouts of kissing in darkened rooms. They were about almost getting caught by parents. At the parties maybe there was beer, maybe pot, probably cigarettes, so you could learn how to drink stuff and smoke stuff, things you needed to know for high school. Maybe you'd get fallen in love with at a party—and everybody wanted a chance to get fallen in love with—or maybe you'd find someone really special. Mikey and Margalo collected stories about the parties, and rumors, and reports, and they considered them. "I don't believe her, do you?" Margalo would ask, while Mikey fulminated, "Catch *me*."

Another useful source of information was Mikey's mother, the ex-Mrs. Elsinger, once again Ms. Barcley. Margalo had elevated Ms. Barcley to an educational experience, so she kept herself current with what Mikey's mother was getting up to, at work, at play. "Did you talk to your mother this weekend?" she asked.

"I was watching the Australian Open."

This did not interest Margalo. She'd already heard her fill on that topic from Mikey. Also, it did not answer her question. "But did you talk to her?"

"She's still crazy about this new boyfriend."

"She's always crazy about them, isn't she?"

"It's just my father she couldn't be in love with," Mikey observed.

"You know, all of these boyfriends have been rich and ambitious and already successful, which your dad just isn't. If you think about them, they drive late-model cars, dress in suits and polish their shoes. They take her to four-star restaurants, they take her away for fancy weekends—your dad didn't do any of those things."

"I just wish she didn't make me meet them."

"Mudpies, Mikey. You're always talking about the places you eat at."

"Besides, this one's much older than she is."

Margalo stared at her friend, who was being the same person she had always been, irritable and impatient and self-confident. *Who cares?* about summed up Mikey, in a plaid flannel men's shirt (a new fashion low for Mikey) and her baggy cargo pants (a long-gone style, but Mikey either hadn't noticed that or—more likely—didn't care). Not noticing things was a big part of Mikey, especially things having to do with people. Margalo knew this about her friend, and sometimes she was really grateful for it. Like now, in the matter of this . . . *thing* that was such a big secret part of Margalo's life, ruining it and making it wonderful. After a minute of staring she told Mikey, "People can love people who are older than them," adding for safety, "or younger."

"What do *you* know about it?" Mikey demanded.

"More than you think," Margalo answered.

"And what's that supposed to mean?" Mikey demanded.

Margalo wasn't about to answer that question. Instead, she said, "Your mother keeps having serious relationships. Do you think she's having sex with all of them? Do you think she's in love with all of them?"

"Dad hasn't had even one girlfriend," Mikey said.

8

"I don't think you *can* fall in love that often," Margalo decided.

"He's been fixed up. People saying, come for dinner to meet, come to a party to meet. But he hasn't been on a date he asked someone out on," Mikey said. "Not a date of his own."

"Not really in love," Margalo said.

"Do you think there's something wrong with him?" Mikey asked.

"I think there's something wrong with *her*," Margalo said.

"You know, you probably won't get the part," Mikey said. "Jennet Whoever."

"Thank you for your kind wishes."

"Get real, Margalo. Do you expect me to want you to? You *know* that if you're in the play, you'll be rehearsing all the time, from now until the performance. Which isn't until May."

"But you're in basketball anyway, or tennis, so why should you care?"

"Because if you're rehearsing, who'll sell our Chez ME cookies?" Last year, after the success of Mikey's cookies in the seventh-grade bake sales, Mikey and Margalo had continued baking and selling cookies. They liked being in business. Margalo welcomed the income and Mikey welcomed the work. It didn't suit Mikey's plans to have Margalo be unavailable for the spring cookie business. "*And* you won't be able to see my tennis matches," she added. "After I make the team. Again."

That *again* made them pause to smile at each other. After brief and unspoken mutual congratulations and admirations, they got back to their quarrel.

Margalo said, "I can do more than one thing at a time, you know."

"And baby-sitting jobs too? That's three things."

"I can count," Margalo said.

"I guess you're pretty confident," Mikey grumbled.

"You're the one who keeps telling me to think like a winner."

"I never said *you*," Mikey objected. "I meant *me*."

Margalo gathered up her lunch wrappers and put them into the brown paper bag. Mikey piled her dirty dishes back onto the tray. But neither one of them made a move to get up. They were in no hurry to get to an all-school assembly.

"So if you do get this part, do you have to kiss someone?"

"What is this sudden interest in kissing?" Margalo asked.

"What makes you so sure you'll be picked?" Mikey asked.

"I'm not." The only thing Margalo was sure of was that she could hear Jennet Jourdemayne's voice in her head, speaking the lines in a cool-headed, intelligent, courageous way. She hadn't even thought of trying out until Mr. Schramm told her she reminded him of Jennet Jourdemayne. Mr. Schramm had been in a production of *The Lady's Not for Burning* out in Oregon, he'd said; he'd played Thomas Mendip; this was before he became a family man and turned in his actor's equity card for a teaching certificate. He was glad to see that they were still reading it in schools, he told her. But didn't she have a class to get to? He wouldn't want to make Margalo late for class, he'd said, and asked, why didn't she try out for Jennet?

"What if you don't get it?" Mikey asked. "What if Ms. Larch picks someone else? Like, Rhonda," she suggested, naming one of their long-time favorite people to dislike.

Margalo had the answer. "Then I'll have more time to sell cookies, which means I'll have more money in the bank."

"Although you'll still have to do something for the play. All eighth graders do. I'm going to be an usher."

"Usherette."

"Usheress."

"In a little short, swishy skirt," Margalo said, grinning.

"I'll swish you," Mikey said.

"You'll need to style your hair, like, curl it for an updo. I'll help," Margalo offered.

Mikey's hand went up protectively to the thick braid that had finally gotten back to long enough, almost halfway down her back. "No way."

"You'll be adorable," Margalo promised—and they both started laughing. *Mikey* and *adorable* were vocabulary words from two different languages. Two different languages spoken on two different planets.

"You should usher too," Mikey suggested.

"Ush," Margalo corrected.

"When you don't get the part. It's a minimum-stress

assignment, and minimum time commitment. Unless—would they give you one of the other parts? Is there another part for someone tall and skinny?"

"Jennet is the only part I want."

"You *could* play a man," Mikey suggested. This was not meant to be flattering.

"It's too bad you didn't have the nerve to try out," Margalo said.

"I thought about maybe that little priest, the one with his lute, the spacey one."

Margalo believed that the best revenge was a quick one. She said, "I guess, because he's supposed to be so short and round, you thought you'd look right."

"Also besides, I don't have time to learn lines. I'd have to miss a lot of practices and also I don't want to let the team down by not playing in a basketball game because of some rehearsal. Also, tennis begins in March, and I'm not about to miss that. So it's not that I didn't have the nerve," Mikey said, with her *I-guess-I-win* smile.

Margalo's attention had moved on to the new problem: If she didn't get the part, she *was* going to have to do something else for the play. Every student in each grade—and every teacher, too—had to do something for the West Junior High School annual class projects, the dance given by the seventh grade for eighth graders, and the play given by eighth graders for everyone. She was about to ask Mikey about the ushering committee, when Tanisha Harris pulled out one of the empty chairs—there were many to choose among near Mikey and Margalo—and sat down in it.

Tan was the only girl as serious about sports as Mikey. In grade school, when they first met her, she was serious about volleyball, but since last year she'd been serious about basketball instead. Tan had a good chance at an athletic scholarship for college, since she was a really good athlete, and smart enough, and African American. She looked at Margalo with dark, measuring eyes and said, "I've got bad news. Do you want to hear it?"

"How bad?" Margalo wondered.

"Not bad like your dog died. This is like—a dead-goldfish level of badness," Tan said. She had always run closer to their wavelength than other people. "It's like a you'll-hate-dinner—it's on a liver-for-dinner level."

"I don't mind liver," Mikey objected.

"OK," Margalo decided. "Tell."

"My grandmother loves it," Mikey told them.

"You know that today in assembly they're announcing who got parts in the play?" Tan asked.

Margalo nodded.

"Sautéed, with onions and red wine," Mikey said.

"I know who's going to be Jennet Jourdemayne. Sorry, but it's not you."

"Hah!" Mikey crowed. All victories welcome, that was her motto.

"Hunnh," said Margalo. She was cool, nothing surprised her, nothing got her excited, nothing could upset her or disappoint her.

"I told you so," Mikey said.

"*Mikey*," Tan protested.

"Well I did," Mikey maintained.

Tan grinned. "You're so bad, you're perfect."

Mikey smiled right back at her, a *So-what?* smile.

"How'd you find out?" Margalo wanted to know.

"The way they're announcing it, they're calling the people up onto the stage. I guess they think that'll make it more exciting for everyone, like the Oscars or something. Aimi told me. She's going to be Jennet. Ms. Larch told her yesterday so she'd be ready to be called up on stage, and Aimi was too excited not to tell someone." Tan continued, "I thought you were just as good as Aimi in tryouts. You're a good liar, so it makes sense that you'd be a good actress."

"Aimi must have been better," Mikey pointed out. "Otherwise, why would she get the part?"

"She's black." Tan made a point of not adding *dummy*, made such a big point that she might as well have said it out loud, which was exactly her point. "Except for that, Aimi and Margalo are built a lot alike, tall and slim, and they're both pretty enough. The only real difference I can see is Aimi's not white. So, I figure, Ms. Larch wanted someone who looked different from everybody else for Jennet, because . . . People in those days would single her out and believe she might be a witch *because* she looked different—when they were looking for someone to blame, for a scapegoat when things went wrong."

"That's smart casting," Margalo agreed.

"Did she tell Aimi all that?" Mikey asked.

Tan just looked at her, eye sarcasm.

"Yeah, but then how do *you* know?" Mikey insisted. Then she said, "Wait. OK. I do get it." In case they didn't believe her, she explained. "The play's set in the Middle Ages, and the Middle Ages are a lot like junior high. The Middle Ages are the junior high of history. In both places, if you look different, or act different, people are nervous, scared of you. Get people scared of you and they'll start doing things to make themselves feel un-scared, like—burning you at the stake. It's as simple as math: Different is scary, new is scary, change is scary—burn, burn, burn." Each time she said *burn*, Mikey pointed at Margalo or Tan, as if she was sentencing somebody to be tied to a stake and roasted alive. "I'll tell you what scares *me*," she said, as if either Margalo or Tanisha had asked. "People."

"The Salem witch trials weren't during the Middle Ages," Margalo pointed out.

Mikey ignored her. "By 'they' I mean mostly men," she said. "Because women couldn't do much of anything back then. Well, they could, and some of them did. Joan of Arc, for example, and look what happened to her because she acted different from other people, and looked different, especially dressed different. Things haven't really changed at all since then, have they?"

Margalo considered deflating this R&R, which was what her mother called it when Mikey got going on some topic, because it was the opposite of Rest and Recreation. With Mikey, Aurora maintained, R&R stood for Rant and Rave. Margalo was about to advise Mikey to put a lid on it, when Frannie Arenberg, who'd stopped on her way out of the cafeteria to listen, did it for her. "I think the human race has made some good progress since the Middle Ages," Frannie said.

"Yeah, but you also think Louis Caselli isn't so bad," Mikey pointed out.

"That's because Louis has a giant crush on her," Tan said.

Frannie never minded being teased, not about her plain, Quaker style of dressing, not about her reputation as the nicest person in school, not even about Louis Caselli's crush. She said, "I feel sorry for Louis."

"Louis has the brains of a mushroom," Mikey agreed. "We have to forgive him. At least," she added, "the rest of you have to. I don't think I will."

"Besides, as we all know, Louis is no competition for . . ." Margalo lingered on the silence before she uttered the name in a breathless, sighing voice, "Gregory Peck." Frannie's crush on Gregory Peck had begun when they'd been shown the movie of *To Kill a Mockingbird* last year. She didn't care if he was old enough to be her grandfather—or great-grandfather by now; and Margalo did agree that he was incredibly handsome. But there was old, and there was way old, and Gregory Peck was definitely in the second category.

As soon as Margalo mentioned the one, Mikey leaned toward Tanisha to murmur the name of the other: "Tiger Woods." In eighth grade you wanted to be half of a couple, so if they didn't have a personal boyfriend, girls could get crushes on celebrities. The important thing was to have a name linked to yours. Almost all eighth graders were linked to someone. Not Mikey, and not Margalo, and there were a few others, too, although not many. Casey Wolsowski was one of these—unless you counted linking your name up to the hero of some book, which most people didn't. This far into the year everybody knew about Frannie's crush and Tanisha's ideal man, so they got teased a lot.

Frannie and Tan looked at each other. "Their time will come," Tanisha promised.

"In your dreams," Mikey answered, and Margalo let Mikey speak for her in this, as if she and Mikey were in exactly the same position, untouched, and untouchable.

"Anyway, I'm not about to waste time and erasers on a notebook," Mikey declared. Eighth-grade girls erased their boyfriends' initials onto the fronts of their spiral notebooks. It was practically an eighth-grade art form, initialing anything you could get an eraser on. "Haven't you seen Ronnie's notebooks, with Doug's name all over them? And Rhonda—it's pitiful. *She's* pitiful. She always was, but this year she's reached new levels of pitifulness. Or Heather McGinty, the way she drools around after whoever scored highest in the last game, whoever everybody's talking about. Acting like she's some movie-star irresistible sex goddess, hinting about how hot she is." Mikey concluded this R&R, "The whole thing's—it's really embarrassing, and Heather's not even embarrassed."

Then she grinned. "I'm enjoying eighth grade."

Then she glared at Frannie. "What's so funny?"

Frannie stood up, shaking her head. "I have to get an aisle seat for the assembly," she apologized, "because I got a part."

"Which one?" Margalo asked, making a silent guess, *The mother*.

"The mother," Frannie said.

"Typecasting," Mikey announced.

"No it isn't," Margalo said. "The mother isn't—"

Mikey held up both hands, palms out like a policeman facing traffic, *Stop*. "Leave me something to be surprised at, why don't you? Who else got parts?" she asked Frannie.

"I thought you wanted to be surprised. Anyway, we're not supposed to tell," she added, leaving.

"Are you trying to get rid of the few friends you have?" Tan asked Mikey.

"What did I do to you? I just said his name, just Tiger. Ti-ger, Ti-ger." Mikey ducked out of Tanisha's reach. "I didn't say anything about, That's a weird name, or, How dumb is it to think you're in love with some sports hero who never even heard of you and never will."

18

"No different from a movie star or a rock star," Tanisha maintained.

But Margalo disagreed. "Tiger Woods is a whole different story from Tyrese." Then she was diverted. "Denzel Washington. I could go for Denzel Washington."

"Or Will Smith," Tanisha agreed.

Mikey groaned. They ignored her.

Margalo didn't remember when it had become fun to make lists of handsome guys, fun just to think about who should be on the list; but she didn't deny that she enjoyed it. It was more interesting than listing all the boys in your class, ranked in order of who you'd like to kiss, or go on a date with, or marry, which one you'd most want to be marooned on a desert island with, or—this was the currently popular list—dance with, or slow dance with or super slow dance with, which were all the same unspoken question: *Who do you want to go to the dance with? If every boy was going to ask you, who would you choose?*

As some art-room kids passed by, Cassie Davis—front-runner for the title of eighth grader with the worst attitude—stopped to ask Mikey, "You coming to assembly? Or what?"

"Is there an *or what* choice?" Mikey asked, then "I'm not joking," she protested.

"I know," Cassie said. "That's what makes you so funny."

"I'm not funny," Mikey told her.

"I'll save you a seat," Cassie said, passing on by.

"Why does she think because we're in the same home-room, she should save me a seat?" Mikey demanded.

"She doesn't mean it," Margalo explained. "She won't do it."

"Then why does she say she's going to? People," Mikey said, disgusted.

Being disgusted with people reminded her of something else. "What committee are you going to be on for the play?" she asked Tan.

Tan was rising, and it really was time to start over to the auditorium. She said, "Promotion—you know, getting advertisers for the programs, finding stores that'll let us put up posters. The committee only meets during lunches, and we can sign up the advertisers and ask at stores during the weekends. It's Mrs. Sanabria's committee so you know it's not going to interfere with the basketball schedule," she said as she joined up with Ronnie Caselli and others from the team.

Watching the cafeteria get empty, Mikey looked at Margalo and smiled, a grim *Let's-look-for-a-bright-side* smile. "The sooner it starts, the sooner it'll be over."

Like someone about to step into the dentist's office, Margalo tucked her straight, chin-length hair behind her ears and squared her shoulders. "If you say so." She rose from her seat.

Slowly, reluctantly, they got going, drifting out of the cafeteria, drifting down the hallways, drifting into the auditorium, just two jellyfish riding along on tidal waters.

# 2
# *LOVE AT FIRST SIGHT*

With the seventh and eighth grades both present, the auditorium aisles were clogged with students, especially the narrow passages separating the rows of seats. People yelled greetings to one another, yelled responses back, gathered together to talk. Groups lingered in the aisles and individuals moved back and forth along the rows. Seated students leaned forward across seats, leaned backward or sideways, whispering for private conversations, speaking loudly if they wanted to be overheard, shouting if they felt like it. Everybody looked around to see who everybody else was talking to, sitting with, looking at.

As Margalo predicted, Cassie hadn't saved Mikey a seat. Mikey and Margalo checked in with their homeroom teacher then took seats directly behind Cassie. Orange streaks in Cassie's artificially black hair were the only color she wore; the rest was black and shapeless—black sweatshirt, black

21

sweatpants tucked into thick black socks. Cassie turned around to greet them ("Whazzup?") and to not wait for a response—which made sense since it had been practically all of four minutes, maybe eight, since they'd last met. "This is just like the Oscars isn't it?" Cassie said. "Or would you say it's closer to Cannes?"

"Give it a rest, Cass," the boy next to her said, twiddling the two silver rings in his right ear. Jason, who wanted people to call him Jace, was Cassie's boyfriend and had been since the start of the year, when a boyfriend, or girlfriend, became as necessary to your public image as having shaved legs or a good working vocabulary of dirty words. Couples littered eighth grade like loose trash in a vacant lot on a windy day—somebody always getting together or breaking up with somebody else, giving everybody else something to observe and talk about, creating a constant need for new notebooks on which to erase newly paired initials.

Mikey and Margalo slouched down in their seats, backpacks on their laps, paying no attention to anybody around them (Mikey), and paying surreptitious attention to everybody, students *and* teachers (Margalo). The 431 students (allowing for a probable absentee rate of about 5 percent) settled down as soon as the principal appeared.

Mr. Saunders ascended the four steps leading up to the microphone. He ran his glance over the audience until the students got quiet, and quieter, and finally fell into a resigned silence. Mr. Saunders was good at principaling, but boring at assemblies. He always started out with the same announcements about upcoming meetings and events, then repeated his same concerns, about littering, about school spirit, about supporting your teams, about taking responsibility. But he coached the school's two best teams, soccer and baseball—the best, some people said, only if you didn't count girls' teams, or the tennis team—and he kept things running smoothly at school; also, he seemed to think students were OK, mostly.

Mr. Saunders made his announcements and then talked about the scores of last Friday's basketball games, praising the teamwork of the players, claiming, "Winning isn't everything, people."

Mikey, who disagreed, grunted. Margalo, who didn't want Mr. Saunders noticing them, jammed her elbow into Mikey's arm. Mikey turned her head, just slightly, just enough so Margalo could see the smile she had put on, or at least half of it; and half of that *I'll-get-you-later* smile was enough for Margalo. She retracted her elbow.

Then came the speech about litter in the bathrooms. Mr. Saunders didn't mention food throwing in the cafeteria or smoking; he didn't need to because everybody knew that when you indulged in either one of those errors in behavior, you were out the door—*boom*—immediate suspension—*boom, boom*—your parents arriving to take you home while you were still trying to think up a good excuse. "I run a tight ship," Mr. Saunders assured them, his usual speech conclusion. "And that's the way I like it. So straighten out, people. Straighten out and fly right."

Next, he praised the seventh-grade bake sale offerings—although they weren't half as good as last year's, as every eighth grader knew—and at last he said, "I know how everybody is looking forward to the dance, but don't forget—we also have a play to look forward to, and today our director is ready to announce her cast. Ms. Larch?" he called, looking out over the auditorium as if the drama teacher weren't already planted in the front row, having given responsibility for her homeroom—this was Margalo's guess—to handsome Mr. Schramm.

Ms. Larch taught C-level English classes to the seventh grade and a creative writing class at each grade level, and she was responsible for Drama Activities. She dressed droopy dark—dark reds, dark browns, dark greens and golds—and she draped scarves around herself, keeping them in place with long, old-fashioned hat pins. She wore beginner ballet slippers, with an elastic across the top. She took the microphone from Mr. Saunders and stood alone on the stage, silent, for a long moment, smiling down on her audience. Then, "Well," she said.

Ms. Larch had been a real actress. She'd appeared on a television soap opera and once had a part in a play that went from Boston to New Haven to Broadway, where it stayed for fourteen months. Her voice was low and husky, like she was a singer in a nightclub. The microphone carried her voice close to each person in her audience, making her public speaking sound like private conversation. It was Ms.

Larch's voice that convinced people she really had been a professional actress. "Lieblings," Ms. Larch said, spreading out her arms in welcome.

"I'll liebling *you*," Mikey muttered. "Frankensteins is more like it."

"Frankenstein was the doctor," Margalo pointed out quietly. "You're thinking of Frankenstein's monster. What you should say is, Frankenstein's monsters, in the plural."

Muffled laughter spread out around them—of which they were not unaware.

"Oh, what a day this is!" Ms. Larch spread her voice as wide as her arms, to encompass everyone. Then she took a deep breath to announce, "As you know, the eighth grade will be giving two performances of *The Lady's Not for Burning*. This will not be until May, so lest you forget, I ask you to mark it on your calendars. Tell your parents, your friends and relations. The play we have selected is a modern comedy"— Ms. Larch waited for the seventh-grade boys to subside ("Phew, not Shakespeare")—"and a romance," she said, her glance daring anyone to say what they were thinking, "about witch hunts." ("All *right*.") "It's a play about being different, about the good and the bad in human nature, and about truths that live deep in the human heart."

"I thought she said comedy."

"I thought she said romance."

Ms. Larch ignored the malcontents. "Only the eighth-grade A-level English students have read *The Lady's Not for*

*Burning,* and they have promised not to give away the story. Let our actors tell the tale, when their time comes. The only thing I will add now, to whet your appetites, is that it takes place in approximately 1400 A.D.—or if you prefer, M.E., modern era—"

"I always prefer m-e," Mikey said, and dodged Margalo's elbow.

"—in a small English village at the very end of the Middle Ages, or if you prefer, the very start of the Renaissance, so there will be wonderful costumes with swords, doublets, long gowns for the ladies, high boots for the gentlemen." Her hands flowed, describing these words with gestures. "Lieblings," she assured them, "I promise you a rare treat." She smiled down on all of them with barely contained excitement.

"I have to admit, I'd've liked you to be a star in this play," Mikey said. "I'd have liked one of us to. It's a fame and fortune op. Well," she amended, "fame, anyway."

Margalo shrugged, as if she didn't care. And, really, she didn't. Really, in fact, she had been satisfied to read Jennet Jourdemayne's lines in the tryout, and imagine Thomas Mendip. She could still feel how it felt that day, hearing her own voice, saying to her imagined companion, "I have come suddenly upon my heart, and where it is I see no help for." She could still imagine him standing close before her. Until she tried out for the role of Jennet Jourdemayne, Margalo had not known how powerful imagination could be, how delicious—as real—almost—as dreams.

26

Margalo brought her attention back to Ms. Larch, who was saying, "I know how eager you are to hear who my co-conspirators in this production will be, and we're ready to confess all." She laughed lightly at her own joke. "So now I'll call on my actors to come and join me here on the stage. But I will not name their roles or give away their parts in the story. Let some mysteries remain, I say. So that we might be open every day of our lives to surprise, and so that curiosity may not die out in us."

"What's *wrong* with the woman," Mikey demanded, but in a muted voice. "Hasn't she ever heard of less is more?"

"Maybe she thinks less can't be more," Margalo suggested.

"Maybe she doesn't think," Mikey suggested.

"Maybe she likes the sound of her own voice," Margalo suggested.

"Maybe she should be struck dumb," Mikey said. "By which I mean 'mute.' Because she's already dumb. *Now* what's got you going?" she challenged Margalo.

Ms. Larch interrupted them, calling: "Louis Caselli." Louis strutted from his aisle seat down to the steps, strutted up the steps, but then ruined the effect by stumbling. He staggered into place onstage. Once there, he grinned, a stocky figure in full-legged jeans, Airwalk sneakers, and an outsize T-shirt, entirely pleased to have everybody's attention.

His name and approach had been accompanied by surprised murmurs ("Caselli can't act, he can't even act like a human being") and cries of encouragement from his friends

("Go get 'em, man"); then there was laughter as he staggered, stumbling, strutting to center stage. "Take your bow, Louis," Ms. Larch reminded him. Louis almost fell over as he bent from the waist while still trying to look up and see how everybody was looking at him.

"Hadrian Klenk," Ms. Larch said next. "You come on up here right now, Hadrian."

Hadrian, who was younger than anybody else in the eighth grade, looked lost as he approached the steps. He looked totally confused. Some people groaned softly, which was the usual response to Hadrian Klenk. If there was a wrong way to do something, Hadrian Klenk found it. If there was something useless to say, that's what Hadrian said, and in a weird, creaky voice you couldn't ignore. The groans got shushed—some people really *did* try not to be mean to Hadrian—as he got up to the stage and started wandering off to stand, wavering a little, beside the teacher. Ms. Larch whispered something to him, and Hadrian drifted over toward Louis.

"What is that kid *taking*?" was one question and "Why would she choose Hadrian?" was another.

At that point Hadrian seemed to become aware that there was an audience, and he bobbed his head at them.

Margalo, who thought she had figured out Ms. Larch's casting choices, wanted to applaud Hadrian; he was exactly right for the little priest.

The next names puzzled her, partly because they were

28

paired, but mostly because they were girls, and if Margalo was correct in her guess, they should have been boys. "Rhonda Ransom—"

"Oh, good," Mikey said.

"—and Heather—"

"McGinty, say McGinty," Mikey pleaded, but she was doomed to disappointment.

"—Thomas."

"Who's Heather Thomas?" Mikey asked as two girls marched together down the center aisle while many voices called out congratulations to them.

"A friend of Casey's from the other A-level English class. She likes Ralph. You remember Ralph."

Mikey did. "Ralph was an OK fighter." She thought. "I'd have won if Mr. Saunders hadn't stopped it," she maintained.

That was last year's fight over last year's issues and not current news. Margalo stuck to the current. "Last weekend he asked Heather to go to the dance with him," she reported.

"Why do you even *want* to know these things?" Mikey demanded.

While they held their low-voiced conversation, Rhonda and Heather Thomas ascended the steps together, one big and blonde, the other just as blonde but shorter, slimmer, overall smaller. They moved in unison without looking at each other, like two coaches, each one of whom thinks he is the best coach of the most important sport. They walked together like two girls, each one of whom thinks she is the one everybody is looking at and wants to date, but doesn't want to hurt her friend's feelings by saying so. They crossed the stage together, to stand together by Louis and Hadrian. They bowed minimally, just a little nod of their heads; they were too important to offer the audience more than that.

"Ira Pliotes and Jason Summerton," Ms. Larch called out, two names that met with general approval, including Mikey's and Margalo's. Ira, who had been in their class since fifth grade, was a pretty well-liked boy, pretty smart, a pretty good athlete; he got along with pretty much everyone. People clapped for Ira, and for Jason, too, since Jason was one of the coolest of the cool and did glamorous things like summer camp in Canada and winter holidays in the Bahamas. Jason was stuck up, no question, and Ira was about the opposite; what they were doing paired up like this was a puzzle. They pushed against each other as they went up the steps and didn't stop the jostling when they stood side by side on the stage. They had to be the quarreling brothers in the play, Margalo thought.

"Frannie—" Ms. Larch didn't finish the name before the applause began as Frannie walked up onto the stage in a stately manner. "—Arenberg."

Of course they all knew that Frannie was their age, fourteen, and an ordinary eighth-grade girl, except for being nice and really meaning it. They were used to the plain way she dressed, because Quakers are plain people in their dress as well as their beliefs, and the styleless style in which she wore her wavy brown hair, parted at the side and held off her face with a barrette, never longer than her chin or shorter than her ears. They all knew Frannie Arenberg, and they knew she was good at math *and* English, science *and* seminar, *and* sports, in the same including way she was popular with both girls and boys, coaches and teachers. They all knew her and counted her a friend, but seeing her onstage was different. She looked like somebody's mother or a vice principal.

"This is like . . . it's like some time warp," Margalo said. "I feel as if I'm seeing into the future. What if this is some science fiction experiment, where going up on this stage shows people as they really, *really* are? Or who they *will* be? I wonder what we'd look like up there."

"Who cares?" Mikey asked. Then she gave herself away by saying, "Louis looks totally sketchy."

"If Louis ends up an alcoholic, would you be surprised?" Margalo asked.

"Just as long as he doesn't end up living next door to me," Mikey said.

"And Rhonda—it's like we're seeing who she'll be when she's thirty. She's like her mother, isn't she? She's all . . ." Margalo tried to think of the words.

"*I know the right way to act,*" Mikey supplied. "*You had all better behave.*"

Margalo finished it. "*Or I'll get you in trouble, because I know important people.*"

31

"Hadrian, at least, doesn't make me want to leave town. He reminds me of Piglet."

"Sweet and helpless."

"But nobody could be that innocent in eighth grade," Mikey decided.

"Somebody two years younger could be."

"Mudpies, Margalo. Remember us in sixth grade?"

Margalo didn't bother arguing. Besides, Mikey was right. So Hadrian was pretending, up there, acting his part, and nobody doubted him—and that was a curious thing, now that she thought of it. If Hadrian Klenk could act, that meant he could probably lie, too—curiouser and curiouser.

"I wish I *had* gotten the part," Margalo said to Mikey. "You could have told me what I look like, up on stage."

"I can tell you now: like a beanpole. An overdressed, underfed beanpole." Then Mikey had a better idea. "Or a praying mantis. Have you ever heard what they do to their mates?"

Margalo jabbed at her twice with a bony elbow, once for *beanpole*, once for *overdressed*.

"They eat them," Mikey said.

Margalo jabbed again and caught her in the ribs.

"After," Mikey said.

Jab.

"Starting at the head," Mikey concluded, blocking the last jab with her arm.

At this point Ms. Larch emptied the stage, sending the

seven actors back to their seats before she announced the final four parts, the four biggest roles. First she called Melissa Martinez, who had dark eyes and long brown hair. Melissa had many wanna-be boyfriends in the eighth grade, even though the rumor was that she already had one, from summer camp. There was a lot of applause and a few whistles for Melissa, who curtsied shyly.

Next, Ms. Larch called Timothy Farmer, a quiet, round-headed, blushing boy, the kind of boy who would never even dare to *think* about having a crush on Melissa. Margalo thought that they must be playing the young couple, and that maybe Ms. Larch was someone who knew how to pick the right people for a play.

"Aimi Hearn, you're next," Ms. Larch called, and stepped forward to hold out her hand to the tall, dark-skinned girl who had taken Margalo's part. Aimi approached the stage and ascended the stairs, like a model or a queen or a dancer, with her long back straight, her head high, proud.

"What do you know about her?" Mikey whispered to Margalo.

"Not much. She keeps to herself. She plays baseball."

"You mean softball."

"She looks like she might be interesting," Margalo said just as Ms. Larch summoned up the last member of her cast.

"Shawn Macavity. Show your face up here, young Shawn."

Who? Shawn who? For a minute, nobody remembered any Shawn Macavity.

An uneasy silence rose up from the gathered seventh and eighth graders, who turned to their friends in puzzlement, then looked around to figure out who this person might turn out to be, to see who was getting up and starting down the aisle.

Ms. Larch started clapping her hands to fill the silence, and Mr. Saunders joined in, and a few of the students, too, the kind of people who always clap first and ask questions later. But the clapping faded quickly as a boy came striding down the center aisle, a dark-haired, long-legged boy in black jeans and a pale, old blue work shirt. He took the steps two at a time, nodded briefly to Ms. Larch, and then turned to face the audience.

They started to remember. "Oh, yeah, *him*." "Didn't he used to wear glasses?" "He's in my math class." "He never says a word in class." "I think he was in my grade school—but never in my section." "Who's he hang out with?"

Shawn Macavity could barely keep from laughing as he looked down at everybody and saw how surprised they were. Surprised, and amazed, and stunned, too. *He* wasn't surprised. *He* had expected to see just what he was seeing, first surprise and then—the expressions changing—almost immediately, amazement that they had never before noticed how cool he was.

After a few long seconds, real clapping began.

Shawn Macavity let it go on for the perfect length of time— a slow count to four, or ten, or fifteen—before he smiled, a smile that fell over them like sunshine, no more concerned with them than sunshine is. Then he bowed elaborately, with a broad flourish of his arm, bowed deeply from the waist, like a prisoner about to be executed by a firing squad because he wouldn't reveal the names of the other members of his resistance group. "Don't shoot!" you wanted to cry out, or like Pocahontas with John Smith, run up and throw yourself in front of him, to save him, or to die beside him.

Because Shawn Macavity was handsome. He had dark, dark hair, and skin as white as marble, and bright blue eyes. His nose hooked out, like on an ancient Roman coin. This was the same nose that got him teased when he was younger, like last fall, before everybody could see what a great nose it was, which today they did. When Shawn Macavity smiled carelessly at them from up on the stage, the whole room got brighter and the girls who had boyfriends were sorry. He was so tall—five nine or ten, at least—and so skinny that you worried he wasn't eating enough. He was so confident, and mocking, that you were afraid he'd never look twice at you.

The applause continued on after Shawn's deep bow, as if it had forgotten it was supposed to stop.

Mikey wasn't applauding. For once she had nothing to say. Margalo would have said something to Mikey about her silence, but as the applause was finally dying down Ms. Larch called out one last name—

But there were no more parts in the play—

But the name was hers.

"Stand up, Margalo Epps, and let everyone get a look at you. You're not shy, are you?"

Furious, Margalo stood up. What was Ms. Larch calling on her for? Loam! Compost! Topsoil! This wasn't fair, nobody had warned her, and she hoped her face didn't give away what she was thinking.

"Margalo is going to be my assistant director," Ms. Larch announced. Her dark, dramatically outlined eyes and hoarse, low voice made this a really big announcement. Nobody applauded or said anything. They waited to hear what made it so big. People in the audience turned their attention back to the stage, so only the five people onstage were still staring at Margalo.

Furious, she sat down. She didn't want to be the subject of any big announcement, and especially not of any big unexpected announcement. "What—," she started to ask Mikey, and then, "Assistant director?"

But Mikey was lost in thought. Or lost in dreams. Or just lost, lost in place.

Ms. Larch concluded, throwing her arms out wide, with a rippling of scarves and a falling free of hair, "I am very enthusiastic about this wonderful play with these wonderful actors." She raised her arms above her head and smiled proudly down on everyone, until they started clapping again, so that she would be satisfied enough to leave the stage and let them get on with their lives.

After that Mr. Saunders dismissed them. The audience got up, in a hurry to leave because they were getting five extra minutes of free time before classes started. Talking, shoving, people crowded into the wide aisles.

But Mikey sat.

Like a bump on a log. Like she'd been beaned with a bat. Like a pet rock, a scoop of mashed potatoes, a dead body.

Unlike any Mikey Elsinger that Margalo had ever seen.

As people streamed out of the auditorium the air filled with the sounds of voices and footsteps. Still, Mikey didn't move.

Could Mikey be having a blood clot? Margalo wondered. She was too young for a stroke, wasn't she?

It was as if Mikey had been changed into something entirely different from her usual self, magicked away (but Margalo didn't believe in magic) or stolen out of herself by aliens (but Margalo didn't believe in aliens).

It was definitely different, and it was a little anxiety producing because Margalo couldn't figure it out. She stared at Mikey's expressionless profile and Mikey stared at the stage, where the microphone stood alone. Margalo had no idea what was going on with Mikey. She tried to think what—

And then she knew. It was the only thing that made sense—even if it made no sense at all—and it made her laugh out loud. Here was an unforeseen development, maybe an unexpected calamity. She had no idea how Mikey would react to falling head over heels. She had no idea how Mikey would land after the fall—on her feet, on her head, or in some horrific belly flop.

Margalo's laughter brought Mikey out of her daze long enough to inform her friend, "It's not funny."

# 3
# BEAUTY AND
# THE BEHOLDER

Everybody else had left the auditorium, but Mikey remained in her seat, like a lifeless life-size model. She stared at the empty stage.

Margalo knew pretty much exactly how her friend was feeling, but they had class to get to. "Time's up, Mikey," she said, and stood. "Mikey?" she asked. No response. "Miykee!"

"All *right*," Mikey groused. "I hear you. I don't know what's—" Then her face lit up—she had an idea! It was with this same gleam in her eye that she connected for a cross-court forehand winner. Mikey surged up out of her seat and shoved past Margalo, dumping her backpack on the floor. "See you in seminar"—and she ran up the aisle.

By the time Margalo got to the hall, carrying both of their

backpacks, Mikey had made her way to the front of the flock of girls who hovered around Shawn Macavity like seagulls circling a fishing boat. Most pretended to be doing something else—tying a sneaker, talking to a friend, tidying hair, or even, in one case, reading a book, although that was Casey Wolsowski, and she might not have been pretending.

Mikey, however, didn't pretend anything. She walked right up to ask, "How do you spell your name?"

"M-a-c-" His eyes were sparkling and his mouth couldn't stop smiling, although he lounged back against the wall as if all this attention didn't interest him much. His body language said, *I'm unbelievably cool,* but his face asked, *Isn't this great?* "A-v—"

Mikey didn't let him finish. "I mean the Shawn part. What kind of a Shawn are you?"

"S-h-a-w-n," he spelled agreeably.

"I *knew* you wouldn't be like the rest of them!" Mikey crowed.

Margalo hung back by the auditorium doors, watching this. She didn't want anyone thinking she was included in this scene of mass pursuit, but she didn't want to miss anything either.

"What sport—" was Mikey's next question.

"Listen, Mikey," Heather McGinty interrupted, with such heavy tactfulness that if it had been a tray, it would have taken both her hands to carry it. She stepped close to Mikey, as a friend might step close to give private good advice to stop her friend from making a fool of herself. Heather smiled up at Shawn; they were two superior beings dealing with a dork. "Nobody wants to be pestered with questions," she said to Mikey. To Shawn she explained, "You have to excuse her."

Mikey smiled back at Heather, but nobody would have mistaken it for friendship.

At that sight Shawn backed off from both girls, one step, two. "Hey," he said with a *What-can-a-boy-do?* look around at the watching faces, backing up another step.

Heather followed him, one step, two, three. "Mikey doesn't know anything about guys," she told Shawn, and her eyes promised him without words, *But I do.* She giggled. "She doesn't even like them." *But I do.*

Mikey paid minimal attention to this and shouldered her way in front of Heather, looking right into Shawn's face. "But what sport do you—"

Rhonda Ransom interrupted to advise Shawn, "You better come with me. Before she punches you. You don't want to mess with Mikey."

Shawn shrugged, looked at Rhonda, looked at Heather, looked at Mikey, and shrugged again. "We've got science," he said to Mikey. He was apparently blind to the victory smirk Heather and Rhonda exchanged as they carried him off between them, the three going down the hall like the President and two Secret Service agents. His attendant

40

blondes kept four alert and wary eyes out, warning off anybody who might come too close to their man.

And Mikey just stood, watching. Not making a snide remark. Not even snorting in disgust. Just watching them walk away from her.

*Not Mikey*, Margalo said to herself. She wanted to deny it. But she couldn't. Mikey looked every bit as goopy as the skunk in *Bambi*, or the rabbit—Thumper, that was his stupid name. Margalo could practically see red cartoon hearts circling around Mikey's head. "C'mon, Mikey," she said again. "Let's get going."

At last Mikey registered Margalo's voice and took the backpack Margalo shoved at her. They were going to have to motor to get to their lockers and then the classroom before the bell rang.

As Margalo clanged her locker door shut she heard Mikey ask a quiet question. Usually you could hear Mikey through steel walls, down whole corridors, over tall buildings, but this time Margalo had to turn to face her friend and ask, "What?"

"He's beautiful, isn't he?" Mikey asked again.

Margalo stayed calm. "I don't know about that, but he sure is handsome."

"Who?" Tan wondered as she walked by. She thumped Margalo on the shoulder. "Congrats."

"Shawn," Mikey said, her voice licking the name as if it was some delectibly delicious ice cream cone. "Macavity," she said, and then repeated the whole tasty thing. "Shawn Macavity."

Tan looked at Margalo. "Is she for real?"

Ronnie Caselli joined them to tell Margalo, "I wouldn't want to do it, but you'll be good," and ask, "Mikey? Are you all right? You look weird."

"I'm *great*," Mikey answered goopily.

"Really weird," Ronnie said. "What's wrong?"

"Would you call him handsome? Or beautiful," Mikey answered.

Ronnie didn't even have to ask who. She knew. "Once you look, definitely beautiful. I mean, he's got great hair, and that nose, and his mouth and . . ." She looked at Mikey and giggled in that *I'm-thinking-what-I'm-too-embarrassed-to-talk-about* way, the kind of giggling people do together.

And Mikey did not tell Ronnie to get real. Neither did she stomp on her foot to stop her from being such a typical eighth-grade-girl twit. Instead, Mikey got stone-faced furious. Margalo could guess what her friend was thinking: *Mine.*

Ronnie could guess too, and she didn't stick around to hear about it, not even to say, *Oh, yeah?* Tan went off with her, and Margalo almost went with them. But she didn't.

"What if it only gets more complicated?" she asked Mikey. "People," she explained, although Mikey hadn't asked her what she meant. "School. Life. What if year after year, the older we get, it never gets easier?"

Mikey shrugged; she couldn't be bothered. "I think *beautiful*," she told Margalo.

# 4
# *HE LOVES ME,*
# *HE LOVES ME NOT*

B y the end of the day, Monday, Margalo was thoroughly bored with the topic of Shawn Macavity.

Mikey was not.

"Why don't you know anything about him? You always know about everyone. Do you think he's Irish? Because of the name. There's McDonald's fast food and Macintosh computers, but those aren't Irish, are they? They're Scottish, so do you think he's Scottish? But he has that black hair. Have you ever seen hair so black? I mean, and not dyed. Have you?"

Other people were not so much bored as mocking, because by the end of the day, Monday, word had spread out along the halls, oozing into classrooms and library and gym: *Mikey Elsinger has a major crush on that guy in the play.* Most people agreed, *This is gonna be good,* because *You know what she's like.*

First thing Tuesday morning Louis Caselli came after Mikey

like a pack of hyenas going after the wounded wildebeest on the Discovery Channel. Approaching her locker, he announced, "Mikey and Shawny, they rhyme," and smirked.

"Get lost, why don't you?" Margalo asked him.

Mikey was busy looking up the hall, and looking down the hall, to catch a glimpse of Shawn. She didn't even seem to hear Louis.

"Mikey likee Shawny," Louis said, and exclaimed, "It's poetry!"

Beside him, his cousin Sal chuckled. Another friend, Neal, punched Louis in the arm to express how much fun this was.

Mikey didn't react at all, as if it didn't bother her one bit to have Louis Caselli making fun of her.

Well, it bothered Margalo. "I don't know about you, Louis," she said in a fake-concerned voice. "I worry about you, how you'll survive. You're such a perambulating nit."

Louis tried to figure out if he'd been insulted in an important way, a way that would require him to save face. "Oh, yeah?" he asked. He chose the one-syllable option. "Whaddaya mean, nit?"

"As in nitwit," Margalo told him, and pinched with her fingers in the air over his head. "As in baby lice." By this time more people had gathered to enjoy the encounter, so that when Louis backed away from Margalo's pincering fingers, the onlookers impeded his retreat. "As in pick nits. Pick"— she pincered, picking near his ear—"Pick"—she picked toward his hair. Then she just stood there, smiling down into his red face, and concluded, "I mean perambulating nit."

Louis's mouth worked to come up with a squashing response. "You—," was as far as he'd gotten when the bell rang, and Sal sympathized with his lost opportunity, "Tough luck, man."

It was odd how people resented Mikey's having a crush on Shawn. The Barbies and preppies scorned her for ambition. "As if," they agreed, not caring who could hear them. "As if she has a chance." The jockettes worried that she would lose interest in the basketball team (possible, in Margalo's opinion) or in the tennis team (unlikely): "What about our *games*?" The arty-smarties wouldn't have minded if Mikey got Shawn, because *that* would show everybody, but they hated to see her acting like everybody else: "She can't mean it. Do you think she's scamming us?"

"Better him than me," was the general opinion among the boys. "I wouldn't want Mikey Elsinger after me. Scary."

The only one who didn't seem to mind—or even notice— was Shawn. Overnight, Shawn Macavity had become the most popular boy in school—more popular even than Ralph or Ira or even Jason Johnston, the leading scorer on the boys' basketball team, single-handedly responsible for their 5-1 record. Shawn became the undisputed king of eighth grade, and he took to the role. He was even kingly in the way he ignored the nickname Louis came up with for him, which some of the other boys also adopted by the second day of Shawn's meteoric rise to total popularity. "Mr. Tooth Decay," Louis named him. "Get it? Cavity, get it?"

But Louis did not call Shawn this to his face. To his face Louis and the others asked Shawn, Didn't he want to try out for the baseball team, since he'd given basketball a pass, or for the track team? Or didn't he like sports? Had he ever played a sport? That's right, he took gym, didn't he, what was he, a brain? Was he, like, on the honor roll? They hadn't thought so, but what was it, did he take art? "You're, like, some chick magnet," they told Shawn, and he just grinned, cool, and shrugged his shoulders, careless.

This regal good humor lasted all the way through Tuesday, but by Wednesday, Shawn Macavity expected a little respect from people. After all, he'd landed the big one. He had the starring role.

With Mikey bitten by the love bug, Margalo had no one to compare Shawn-notes with, no one to surprise by the accuracy of her predictions about how long the modesty phase would take to turn into the *I'm-pretty-wonderful* phase, no one to share her desire to prick him like a balloon. Although, she couldn't deny that he *was* handsome; everybody was right about that. Casey Wolsowski declared, "He's what Romeo should look like," and Cassie said almost the same thing, "He's like looking at art."

"Art who?" Margalo asked and "Not funny," was Mikey's

response, then she asked, "What art?" so she could go to the library and look at it.

The good news was: Shawn Macavity didn't have a girl-friend. Which meant: He didn't have a date for the dance. Until he got up on stage on Monday, nobody had particularly noticed him. He never had anything much to say, and he wasn't on any teams. He had nothing to offer a girl, until Monday.

"I'd go to a dance with *him*," Mikey said.

Margalo tried sarcasm followed by insult. "Big surprise. But would he go with *you*?"

Even that didn't get Mikey back to normal. Even Louis couldn't do it, even on Wednesday morning when—with his usual followers—he came up to Mikey's locker and sang, "Way down upon the Shawny River . . ." Or he would have sung it, except Louis couldn't carry a tune. "Far, far away. That's where Mikey's heart is going ever . . ." He cackled with laughter, unable to sing on, doubling over at the sight of Mikey's face.

"You mean Swanee, it's the Swanee River," Margalo told him. "You massive fraculence."

"How do you spell that, Margalo?" one of the boys behind Louis asked.

"Look it up," Mikey suggested. "And I'm getting tired of you," she said to Louis, but she didn't even smile.

"Uh-oh," Louis said, holding up fake trembling hands to fake protect himself. "What're you going to do about it? You

47

aren't going to tell Mr. Tooth Decay on me, are you? He doesn't even know your name."

"Yes he does," Mikey said.

Margalo stepped in. "If you need a more user-friendly word, how about idiot? Does that ring a bell? Synonyms: dolt, dummy, dunce, dullard." She stopped and Louis took a breath, but before he could speak she went on. "Dud, dupe, dingbat." She stopped again.

He opened his mouth.

Before he could say anything, she did. "Dodo."

Louis made a strangled sound, but she cut him off. "Doofus." She thought, then nodded her head. "And that's just the d's."

By then he had turned around and was walking away. "Spanish," she called after him, "*el stupido*. French—" but he was out of earshot, which was lucky because she was out of foreign languages. The bell rang and "What's wrong with you?" she asked Mikey, then, "Why are you putting up with him?"

"What does Louis Caselli matter?" Mikey asked her.


Emboldened by success, at lunch Louis attacked again.

Mikey and Margalo were sitting side by side at their table, just beginning their lunches—Margalo's a tuna salad on lightly toasted supermarket white bread, and Mikey's one of the few popular cafeteria meals, two slices of cheese pizza with a side of french fries. Mikey stared across the crowded room in what Margalo had already identified as her in-the-same-room-as-Shawn-Macavity stupor. Shawn was like the magnet, and Mikey's attention was like the iron filings that line up to point to where the magnet is, if they can't go flying across whatever space separates them to cling right onto it. Mikey sat, and stared, and didn't even know how obvious she was.

No, Margalo corrected herself, biting into the tuna sandwich. Mikey didn't even *care*. Margalo had added a little chopped onion to her tuna salad and she would have offered Mikey a bite, so Mikey could admit that Margalo occasionally had good cooking ideas, but when Mikey was having a Shawn Macavity spasm, there was no getting through to her. She hadn't even taken a bite of pizza, which she usually wolfed right down.

Mikey just sat. And stared. Margalo sighed, a sigh that was half a groan. She ate some sandwich, then groaned, a groan that was half sigh. She wasn't sure how much of this she could take. At last Mikey spoke.

"Why's he talking to Louis?"

Margalo didn't bother asking who. She looked over to where Louis Caselli leaned down over Shawn, and Shawn twisted in his chair to talk up at him. Louis said something, Shawn asked a question, Louis jabbed with his chin in the direction of their table. Before anyone caught her staring at him, Margalo looked hard at her sandwich. Shawn was getting stuck up, just like any overnight rock star sensation, or movie star sensation, or sports star sensation, and Margalo never wanted to contribute to anyone's sense of stuckupedness.

"What's Louis doing?" Mikey asked.

"I thought you didn't care about Louis," Margalo said.

Margalo had asked her mother how long this first, stupefied, phase of Mikey's big crush would last, but Aurora was no help. "Love takes different people different ways," she had said, but Margalo already knew that from her own experience. She announced the obvious. "He's coming over here."

Margalo watched Louis Caselli strut around among the long tables, and she put down her sandwich. It was always good to have your mouth free when you encountered Louis Caselli. She knew it was going to be up to her to take full advantage of this Louis Caselli irritation op, because Mikey barely glanced at Louis before her attention—*Ping! Zip! Zap!*—swung back to Shawn Macavity.

Louis strutted over to stand right in front of Mikey, blocking her view. "Hey!" she protested.

"Hey yourself, Mee-shell," Louis answered, the first time since fifth grade he'd risked calling Mikey by her detested real name.

Then she did look at him. And smiled—a bug-squashing smile.

Louis said, "I was just talking to your heartthrob."

"Go away," Mikey said.

"Mr. Tooth Decay," Louis said.

"Dumb joke," Mikey said.

"Don't you want to know what he said to me?"

"I *want* you to go away."

"Oh, yeah? Well, OK. Maybe I will. Maybe that's just what I will do. I think it is, because I guess you don't want to know what he said when I asked him about you." Louis smirked, strutting in place, turning as if he was about to leave.

"Good-bye, Louis," Margalo said. "Good riddance to—"

"Bad rubbish, ha ha," he cut her off.

"I was going to say, soiled sullage," Margalo answered.

"What do you do, read dictionaries for fun?" Louis demanded.

Then Mikey asked just the question Louis wanted her to. "What *did* he say?"

"Mikey!" Margalo protested.

"Who?" Louis asked, playing dumb now. "What did who say?"

Margalo told him. "You know who."

"Shawn," Mikey said. "Shawn Macavity."

"What about him?" Louis asked, smirking.

Margalo would have liked Mikey to punch that smirk off Louis Caselli's face. He smirked as if somebody having a big crush—a big, hopeless crush—turned that somebody into someone to make fun of. She couldn't believe that Mikey was letting him get away with this.

Mikey gritted her teeth. "What did he say?"

"Say about what?" Smirk.

"About me." Grit.

"Oh, yeah, that. You really want to know?"

Grit.

Smirk.

"Yes! for scum's sake."

"Enough to trade your lunch for the information?"

Margalo stepped in again. "How much information is there? It's not like you were talking very long. I wouldn't do it, Mikey."

"But Mee-shell will. Because she's dying to know what Mr. Tooth Decay said. When I asked him about her."

"I'm not you," Mikey told Margalo as she pushed her tray across the table toward Louis.

Margalo sat back, gave up, and butted out. If Mikey was going to be like this, there was nothing she could do.

The tray rested at the center of the table, with Mikey's hands on one side and Louis's on the other, and Louis's smirking face hanging above it like some baboon hanging down from a branch. "He said," Louis said, "and I will quote his words exactly, because I know you'd like to hear his exact words. He said, and I quote exactly, word for word: 'Who's Mikey Elsinger?'"

Then Louis jerked the tray, fast.

But Mikey was faster. "I don't believe you," she said, pulling it back.

"You made a deal!" Louis protested.

Suddenly Margalo felt much better.

Margalo wasn't the only audience of this little scene. Many

people were curious to see where this would lead, especially those people close enough to listen, and the lunch duty teachers had also taken note. Louis had lost a lot of social ground in the fall, when he decided it would make him popular to jam Hadrian Klenk into wastebaskets whenever he could. After the third jam some of the boys—led by Ira and Ralph, Sean Mitchell and Michael Stone—kept near Hadrian in the halls; and all of the girls refused to speak to Louis, even his cousin Ronnie, who usually felt she had to defend him. Frannie Arenberg, typically, did it differently. She just told Louis to his face that he should be ashamed of himself. It was Frannie's opinion that stopped him. Louis was pretty consistent about what girl he liked (Frannie Arenberg, ever since last year), as consistent as he was about the girls he disliked.

"Cheater!" Louis told Mikey, adding a couple of choices from the list of words Mr. Saunders didn't want to hear spoken in his school. "You traded it to me."

Margalo answered Louis's accusation. "Oh my goodness," she said. "He's right, Mikey. And he clearly *needs* another lunch, the poor little undernourished thing. Otherwise," she added to Louis as Mikey, with perfect timing, let go of the tray, causing Louis to stumble backward and the plate of pizza to leap up at his chest in a mute but effective attack, "otherwise, you might not look so much like an unexpurgated slug."

At first Louis couldn't think of a response. Then he decided he ought to threaten, so everybody watching would know he had the upper hand. "I don't know what you mean by that," he snarled at Margalo.

"No," she answered sweetly. "I didn't think you would."

Mikey had withdrawn from the argument now that she could see the back of Shawn Macavity's head again. But she *had* taken the second half of Margalo's sandwich and was chomping away at it.

In his best *so-there* voice Louis closed the argument. "I didn't think you did."

"I know," Margalo continued it, with more and sweeter patience.

Louis was losing. He didn't know how that had happened. He looked around to the watching faces to tell them, "She's got a crush on Shawn, can you believe it? As if he'd even look at her once." Then he was seized by an unfortunate inspiration. "Or maybe he would. Because pretty guys like him are usually gay, aren't they? And gay guys like—"

Mikey had him by the throat, which limited his ability to verbalize. She was about his height, so he could see right into her eyes. The sight was not pleasant to him.

"Lgo!" he gurgled.

"Don't you ever—," she was starting to say.

Then her words, too, were cut off. Called in by one of the teachers on lunch duty, Mr. Saunders had arrived. He put one hand on Mikey's shoulder, shoving his other arm between the two of them, standing far enough back so that Mikey had time to recognize him and abort the punch she was about to throw at whoever was getting in the way of her choking Louis Caselli to death.

"All right, you two." Mr. Saunders was not amused.

Most of the onlookers, however, *were*. "What is *wrong* with Louis?" people wondered, and "What is *wrong* with Mikey?" People also thought, *Why don't they grow up?* but nobody said that out loud.

"You know the drill," Mr. Saunders told Mikey and Louis.

They did. Since September there had been several opportunities for the principal's innovative response to violent eruptions of junior-high tensions, so everybody knew the drill. For the observers the drill was enjoyable and instructive. For the participants it tended to be embarrassing and instructive.

Instructive, and corrective, too; although this time it involved Mikey Elsinger, who never thought she was in the wrong, and Louis Caselli, who never thought. Between them, Mikey and Louis might come up with the disagreement that was the drill-breaker, and nobody wanted to miss that.

Mr. Saunders put one hand on Mikey's left shoulder and one hand on Louis's right shoulder and pushed the two of them in front of him out of the cafeteria. He sent Hadrian Klenk to his office. "Get me the gloves," he told Hadrian as he steered his two miscreants down the hall to the gym.

After Hadrian brought the fat brown leather boxing gloves, and Mr. Saunders had laced them on Louis and Mikey, he asked the usual drill questions.

"What's this fight about?" he asked. "Mikey?"

"Ask Louis," Mikey said.

"Louis?"

"It's not my fault."

Mr. Saunders said, "You know we're not looking to assign blame, Louis. We're interested in the cause. We like to know what we're fighting about."

"About name-calling," Mikey said.

"Louis called you a name?"

"I didn't say *one thing* about her."

"You didn't call names?"

That, Louis couldn't deny. But he pointed out, "It wasn't her. So what's her problem?"

"It wasn't you?" Mr. Saunders asked Mikey. "Then who?"

Mikey shook her head.

Hoping to embarrass Mikey, Louis volunteered, "It was her boyfriend."

Mikey smiled a little pleased smile—Margalo could have sworn she saw that—and more than one girl's voice called from the onlookers, "He is not."

"OK, her big crush. Shawn. Macavity. You know," he smirked around at the watching seventh and eighth graders, several of whom groaned softly, hoping that Louis was not going to make this particular joke in front of the principal, under these circumstances, and several of whom hoped that he would. He did. "Mr. Tooth Decay."

Mr. Saunders considered this information before he decided,

56

"I don't need to know just what you said. Although," he warned Louis and everyone else, "I can guess what it might have been. Also," he warned Mikey, "I don't need to hear why you found this enough reason to assault a fellow student."

"Yeah," Louis said.

"But I want you both to take a full minute of silence— everybody silent now, you know the drill—to think about whether or not you want to go ahead with this fight."

"I'm not scared of her." Louis feinted a couple of times. Mikey drew her arm back and punched at his head but Louis danced back, out of reach. She assumed a boxing stance, arms raised and elbows close to her sides, her gloved fists out in front, and jabbed twice at his face.

Whispers spread the question and its answer, "What *did* he call Shawn? Aside from Tooth Decay."

Mr. Saunders cleared his throat.

The whole big, hollow room grew silent. Mikey glared at her sneakers. Louis glared at Mikey, then turned to catch his cousin Sal's eye, then glared at Mikey again.

Mr. Saunders, like an orchestra conductor, kept everybody pretty much quiet together. People were staring at Shawn Macavity; or they carefully didn't even look at him; or they looked at him, then looked away. So everybody noticed when he leaned forward to whisper something to Heather McGinty, who was, as always, positioned right next to him— unless Rhonda Ransom got there first. If you were watching the crowd, as Margalo was, you could see the way what

Shawn whispered snaked forward to the inside ring of students, as Heather McGinty whispered into Rhonda's ear, and Rhonda told Derrie, and Derrie told Lynn, and Lynn told Ira, who told Will, who told Sal.

"Says who?" Sal demanded, too loudly.

"Says who what?" Mr. Saunders asked Sal, checking the clock to see that the minute was as good as up.

"Nothing."

"I'm not buying that, Salvatore."

Sal knew better than to try to avoid answering. "He"—Sal jerked his head back toward where Shawn Macavity was standing—"thinks this is stupid. Not the drill, sir. Everybody likes the drill. He means her. Her fighting about what Louis called him. Because he definitely isn't. But even if he was, he doesn't believe in homophobia. He thinks Louis is having homophobia."

Mr. Saunders looked over at Shawn Macavity, whose alarm at this attention was visible. Then he looked down at Louis and Mikey, and both of their faces were pink, although Louis's was closer to red. Mikey dropped her hands to her sides and shrugged her shoulders. "All right," she said.

"All right?" Mr. Saunders asked, surprised.

"All right I don't want to fight," she told him.

Louis put both of his gloved hands over his head and shook them together, the boxer who just got the decision.

"I'm not apologizing," Mikey told Mr. Saunders.

Mr. Saunders pretended that the topic of apology had

never come up. He unlaced the boxing gloves and pulled them off her hands. Next he turned around and did the same for Louis. "That's it, then," he said. "All right, people, it's time for class."

This was how the drill had always worked out so far; and it had always been something of a disappointment as well as a relief. As if nothing much had happened—and in fact, nothing at all had happened—Mr. Saunders strode to the door, turning there to tell them all, "Let's get going, people. You've got six and a half minutes." But before he left them, he added, "Louis, I want to see you in my office at the end of the day. No"—he held up his hand—"excuses."

This was a variation on the usual final step of the drill. Usually, both combatants were summoned to Mr. Saunders's office at the end of the drill. "What about *her*?" Louis demanded.

Mr. Saunders ignored his tone of voice. "It's you I want to see today."

"Why not her?" Louis insisted.

Mr. Saunders did not like being insisted at. "Because she isn't the person who also trashed another student, more than once, and more than twice, too. I mean, literally trashed."

Louis whipped around to locate Hadrian. "You told! You geek, you squealed!"

Hadrian looked a little pale, but he didn't try to hide. And when he spoke, his voice didn't creak. He sounded like an actor playing George Washington in a patriotic movie, or

Abraham Lincoln, somebody whose word you would never even think of doubting, Harrison Ford. Hadrian's voice sounded deep and grown up, absolutely truthful, and wise, too.

"I wouldn't," Hadrian said.

"Why would I tell?" that voice continued, meaning, *You're so unimportant, why would I bother getting you in trouble?*

"As if," Louis muttered.

Mr. Saunders informed him, "It doesn't matter how I found out, but I can assure you the information didn't come from Hadrian. I repeat, Louis: I expect you at the end of the day. In my office. You'll be there?"

Louis gave up. "Yeah. Is that all?"

"I hope so," Mr. Saunders said, and then he exited the gym through the big doors, with Louis right behind him.

The rest of the students dispersed then, mostly talking about Louis Caselli, if he was a real jerk, or a real rebel, or real stupid, or real brave, or what. They left the gym the way passengers leave an aircraft, some hurrying to be ahead of everyone else, some lingering to be last, and most—absentmindedly—crowding along together between first and last. Mikey lingered, so Margalo lingered with her. Just like last year, they had the same afternoon classes, because they were in the same seminar with the same teacher as last year. Being in the same seminar meant that Mikey and Margalo took earth science together, and the tech courses, too—home ec, industrial arts, computer. Margalo usually reviewed her science notes during those tech classes, while Mikey accused her of trying to get the better grade in science, then went on to accuse her of being overly competitive. "You have everything except math and science to be best at," Mikey reminded her. "Except sports, too," Margalo reminded her, and "Except sports," Mikey agreed. "And cooking." Mikey nodded. "And these tech courses, all of them," Margalo reminded her, but Mikey maintained, "That doesn't mean you can't let me keep science. I don't know what's wrong with you this year. Next thing I know, you'll be in some A-level math class," she said, and they both laughed. Margalo and math began with the same letter, but that was as far as it went.

They had seminar to get to now and books to take from their lockers, but Mikey didn't seem to be in any hurry to leave the gym. She hung around so long that the students from the next class started to drift back into the big room in shorts and T's. Still Mikey didn't get herself out the door, even though this was a boys' gym class—

And then it all made sense to Margalo. "Let's *go*, Mikey," she urged. "I'm going," she announced.

Slowly, Mikey drifted toward the door. Her lingering paid off, because just as they were coming out Shawn was entering. "Hey, Shawn," Mikey said. And stopped.

"Hi," he answered, moving on into the gym.

"See you," Mikey said to his back. She walked on a few slow steps, dragging behind Margalo like some little red wagon. Then she caught up.

61

"He didn't say anything to me," she told Margalo. "I mean, right after. But he had gym to get changed for. But he could have said something. But he did say hi. But he didn't . . ." She was quiet, thoughtful, for a few paces before she asked, "Do you think he'll ask me to the dance?"

# 5
# WHAT IS *THE WAY* TO A MAN'S HEART?

On Friday, an icy cold rain drove down out of the sky. It was not, however, icy enough to close schools, so the day was colored by disappointment. In the cafeteria Shawn Macavity sat with his back to Mikey, not the angle she preferred. Also, lunch that day was tuna noodle casserole with anonymous-fruit crumble for dessert, which did not improve Mikey's spirits, and Margalo's lunch choices had been so limited that she had a peanut butter and jelly sandwich, peanut butter crackers, and no fruit. Lousy weather, lousy Shawn op, lousy food, and only halfway through the day—both Margolo and Mikey were having low spirits.

To speed time along, Mikey and Margalo were making up possibilities for what Mikey's weekend with Ms. Barcley might include (a day at the spa, with facials and pedicures; a day at the office, with video games and being no trouble; shopping for sofa cushions or shoes) and griping about their lunches. Then Tan thwacked a tray of salads—green salad and fruit salad, plus pasta salad for carbohydrates—down onto the table. She slumped into a chair, sticking her long legs out in front of her. She jerked open one of three milk cartons and jammed a straw into it. "I can't take it anymore," she grumbled, and picked up her fork. "We all get warned about the same things about how girls our age change and give up, we all watch the same TV shows, you'd think . . ." She pronged a chunk of cantaloupe and looked across at Mikey and Margalo. "I mean, nobody but me is interested in the team anymore. Me and you, Mikey. You *do* still want to play, don't you?" She studied the orange chunk of melon, looked at Mikey, then at Margalo. "Sometimes I wish I was like you two and didn't care about having friends."

"Is the team mad at you?" Margalo guessed.

"Not me personally. Just mad at what I think. Or, mad at what I don't think. Or maybe because I say what I think? But I'm not one of his fans, so I'm no competition, so they're not mad at *me*. Not exactly. Bored at me is more like it."

"Shawn Macavity," Margalo guessed.

Tanisha nodded.

"The whole team has a crush on Shawn? All of them?" Margalo wondered.

"Except Ronnie, of course. And me," Tan said.

"But what about *me* and Shawn?" Mikey demanded.

"You know what really gets me? What really gets me is the way everybody acts about it. Pretending," Tan grumbled.

Mikey reassured herself. "He doesn't care about sports."

"You mean, talking like friends do?" Margalo guessed. "All supportive? Saying, *He should like you*, when what they're really thinking is *I hope he chooses me*."

"I wouldn't mind if they were like Mikey and had no pride."

"I have plenty of pride," Mikey argued. "But what does that have to do with Shawn?"

Tan had another complaint. "Darlene's asking him to her party tonight."

"She hasn't asked me," Mikey reported.

They didn't say anything. It was too obvious.

"But how will I ever get him to like me if everybody else goes to parties with him and I don't?" Mikey demanded. "I better give my own party."

They didn't bother responding to that, either.

"OK, then, if you don't go to parties with them, how else can you make boys like you?" Mikey asked.

"Who cares?" Tan asked.

Mikey never minded stating the obvious. "I do. That's why I'm asking. What's wrong with you today, Tan?"

Tan reported, "He's not going to Darlene's anyway."

Margalo volunteered, "The way to a man's heart is through his stomach. Steven said that last night, to Aurora, because dinner was so bad."

"He said that?" Mikey asked.

"Of course," Margalo added, "most of Aurora's dinners are pretty lame."

"Do you think he's right?" Mikey asked. She was getting that gleam in her eye.

"It's an old saying," Margalo told her, before she pointed out, "It was a joke, Mikey."

Who cared if it was a joke? Mikey was having An Idea.

"Obviously it's about looks," Tan said. "On TV, in movies—when a guy explains why he's in love, he always says, 'You're so beautiful.' And the most popular girls are the prettiest ones. Like Melissa and Ronnie. Or even Rhonda. I know how you feel about Rhonda, but she *is* pretty. She has that long, thick hair, and it's blonde—OK, but you have to give her a good body. Ronnie's is better, but Rhonda's is"—Tan phrased it delicately—"more noticeable." Then, "C'mon, stop groaning, stop laughing, it's true. C'mon you guys, I mean it."

Margalo and Mikey were hooting with laughter, and Tan eventually joined in. Their loud laughter cut through the other noises in the cafeteria and the two teachers on lunch duty—Mr. Schramm and Mrs. Sanabria that day—looked at each other, wondering if one of them needed to come quiet the girls down, if this noisiness heralded trouble better nipped in the bud than hacked down in full flower. Margalo watched this exchange and saw that when Frannie Arenberg at that moment sat down next to Tan, the two teachers went back to their slow pacing around the cafeteria.

"What's so funny?" Frannie asked them.

Casey slid into the chair beside Frannie and they both waited for the answer to that question. They would go on to seminar together, after lunch, Casey, Frannie, Mikey, and Margalo.

Mikey turned to Frannie. "Did you ever hear that the way to a man's heart is through his stomach?"

"Yes," Frannie said.

"It's an old saying," Casey explained to Mikey.

"Why?" Frannie asked.

"Nothing," Mikey said, but she still had that look in her eye, and that lining-up-a-backhand-down-the-line, going-for-a-winner smile.

"It's because that's the stereotype. Women are supposed to be good cooks," Casey explained. "To be a real woman. Like in the *Little House* books, Ma's a good cook."

"Of course she is, she's the mother," Tan pointed out. "But we're not talking about old-fashioned mothers."

"Although," Frannie argued, "if you think about it, in order to get to be a mother, you have to start with a boyfriend. Someone you might want to—you know—marry, to be the father. So it could help if you show him what a good cook you are."

"*Like Water for Chocolate*," Margalo remembered.

"You saw that?" Casey asked. "That's an R rating."

"The little kids were in bed before we put it on." Margalo called over to Cassie, who was passing by, "Did you see *Like Water for Chocolate*?"

"On video," Cassie said, waving Jace on without her. She joined them at their table. "Great running nude scene. But way unbelievable plot, if you ask me."

"Actually, we were talking about the cooking," Margalo said.

"Didn't believe that, either," Cassie told them.

"I've never seen an R-rated film," Casey said. "My parents won't let me."

"I bet they read you *Grimm's Fairy Tales,* though, didn't they?" Cassie argued. "Really grim, those old Grimm brothers, like when they make Snow White's wicked stepmother put on iron shoes—they've been heated in the fire, too, red-hot iron shoes. And make her dance, at their wedding, isn't it?"

"How would I know that?" Tan demanded. "I just know that the prince falls in love with a dead girl. What's that called, Margalo?"

"Necrophilia," Margalo said.

"Yeah," Tan said. "Yuck."

"She's not really dead," Casey pointed out.

"*He* doesn't know that," Tan argued. "All he cares about is she's beautiful. I *ask* you."

Cassie completed her argument, "They make her dance until she falls down dead."

"They should at least let me watch *Like Water for Chocolate* on video."

"We never watch if it's R for violence," Margalo told the group.

"But you don't even watch the news," Tan said.

"Not the six o'clock," Margalo said. "Not when the little kids are around."

"I don't blame your parents," Frannie said. "Mostly, the news *scares* me."

In life as in tennis, Mikey kept her focus. "Just because everybody says it's only looks that gets boys, that doesn't make it true," she pointed out. "Have any of you asked *them* about it?"

They howled in protest, and laughed at her naïveté, and called loudly over one another's voices, imagining how such conversations might go, which created another round of rowdy laughter from their table, causing more attention to be temporarily paid to it. Mr. Schramm took a couple of steps toward them, then caught Margalo's eye. He smiled, the mischievous smile that always lifted Margalo's spirits. She smiled back. He turned away then, and she wondered why, until she saw him shake his head at Mrs. Sanabria who now stood behind the table where Louis Caselli and his friends sat, a standing warning to the boys that whatever they were thinking of starting had better get itself forgotten.

Once her friends had finished making fun of her, Mikey persisted, "We should ask Ronnie. That's a good . . ." With Mikey, thinking was doing, so she got up to go over to the table where Ronnie Caselli sat among some of the most popular preppies and jockettes, with the other seats occupied by half the boys' basketball team. In Ronnie's whole huge family there was only one girl near her age, her cousin Sophie, a tenth grader—who was, in fact, the person who'd introduced Ronnie to her boyfriend, Doug. Most Casellis were male, which meant—as Ronnie often told them, to justify her popularity with boys, and apologize for it, and boast, too—she understood boys and knew how to get along with them.

While Mikey was gone, Frannie raised a question. "Doesn't there have to be more than just one thing boys like about girls? There is for girls, and boys can't be that different from us, can they? It's not only the good-looking boys who have girlfriends. And besides, nobody has just one reason for doing something. I think there's a lot the same about boys and girls—there has to be, we're all just human beings."

"You believe that?" Cassie asked, doubting. "Do you listen to the way they talk? And do you see the kinds of things they do? And call it fun?"

"Some of them care about other things than looks," Frannie maintained. "Probably a lot of them, if we knew."

"Like intelligence," Casey said. "Being interesting to talk to."

"Who do you think you're kidding?" Cassie laughed.

"Or athletic ability, because then you can understand how they feel about sports," Tan said.

Casey tried again. "In *Rebecca* everybody falls in love with her—even though she's horrible, she's really a horrible person—because she has the *je ne sais quoi*."

"What's that?" Mikey demanded, sitting down again.

Casey hesitated, trying to translate. "*It*," she tried. "You know."

"You mean she slept with them? You mean sex? Can't you speak English?" Mikey demanded.

"I'm sorry," Casey said. "I didn't mean—it's just a French

phrase for—Margalo?" Her eyes filmed with tears. "I read it," she apologized.

"You read too much," Mikey told her. "When you read too much, people look more complicated than they really are. You and Margalo, you both do that."

"Margalo understands people," Casey said, her voice only a little quivery.

"Margalo doesn't know anything about this," Mikey maintained.

Tan disagreed. "She's got brothers, so she knows more than you. Or me."

Mikey said, "Brothers isn't what I meant. I meant *this*." Words having failed her, she jabbed her finger at the place in the cafeteria where Shawn Macavity was moving over to the seat Ronnie was vacating, then jammed the finger into the center of her own chest. "*You* probably think it has to do with earth science," she told Margalo.

In fact, that wasn't what Margalo thought, but she defended the position anyway to see if she could. "Well, it *is* biology. Reproduction. Natural selection and survival of the fittest, and that's Darwin. Breeding for selected characteristics." Groans and laughing protests greeted her argument.

So she continued. "We're animals, after all."

"They're the ones who are animals," Ronnie said, sitting down. "Take it from someone who lives with them. Luckily"—she smiled smugly—"I'm an animal lover."

Cassie pointed out to Ronnie, "They're only animals if you

71

use your looks as bait. I mean, have you seen the way Heather Mac is dressing this week? It's as if—like all of her sweaters got shrunk. At least you don't dress like that," she told Ronnie. "Although, with a bod like yours, you could probably dress the way I do and still get noticed."

"*You* get noticed," Ronnie argued.

"For myself, who I am," Cassie said. "Or my artwork," she added. "But not for my good looks."

"*Nobody* could look good in what you wear," Ronnie said.

"My prune costume, you mean?" Cassie laughed, pulling her black sweatshirt out from her torso to show it off. "It keeps me out of trouble—which is more than those turtlenecks and khakis do for you with the famous Doug, if what I've heard is true."

"And *I* hear Jace doesn't dare try anything with you."

For a minute Cassie glared at Ronnie, then she shrugged. "I guess I'm the new breed, and you're not. Lucky for Doug, isn't it? He's got it easy."

Ronnie snorted, to mean *Ha!* and to say, *You think you're so smart.* She didn't glare; she smiled in a kindly fashion, as if Cassie were her idiot little sister. "Do you really think it's any easier for them than us? If you do, you've got a lot to learn, Cassie Davis." With that line she rose and left their table.

"I plan to be a slow learner," Cassie called after her, then turned to the people remaining at the table. "Things I don't want to get A's in, at fourteen. Number one, sex," she said, counting on her fingers. "You've got the right idea, Casey, falling in love with Maximilian de Winter."

"I'm not in love with him," Casey protested.

"Who?" Tan asked.

"It's that book," Frannie explained. "*Rebecca.*"

"I might have guessed," Mikey said.

"I know the difference between stories and reality," Casey told Cassie.

"But what stories?" Margalo asked. "And whose reality? I mean, I know some people whose reality is pretty delusional," she said. "Ms. Barcley," she named one.

This reminded Mikey, "And I have to go there this weekend. To my mother's," she told the group. "She went back to her maiden name."

"We all know that," Cassie said. "And none of us care. Why should she take her husband's name in the first place, and especially, why should she keep it when they're not even married anymore?"

That subject didn't get discussed, however, because Tan asked, "Has anyone else been asked to this party at Darlene's? Tonight."

"Rhonda's having one too," Frannie said, "and she's got Shawn Macavity coming to it so I expect everybody else will want to. Does Darlene know?" she asked Tan.

"Probably by now she does. Do you think she'll cancel? Maybe not," Tan decided. "I'll still go."

"You're going to Heather McGinty's tomorrow, aren't you?" Cassie asked Frannie, who nodded.

"Me too, oh good," Casey said. "Shawn's going to be there."

Mikey's alarm grew.

"Shawn's going to Rhonda's tonight? And Heather's tomorrow? I wonder if I can get my mom to bring me home Saturday afternoon in time to go to Heather's."

"Were you invited?" Margalo hadn't been.

"Of course not," Mikey said. "She'd never. But that doesn't mean I wouldn't go."

"You'd crash it?" Cassie asked, and when Mikey nodded all she said was, "Cool."

"Shawn's probably why all the parties are happening," Frannie said.

"Well, dunhh," they told her.

"Because he doesn't have a date for the dance," Frannie continued.

"I bet I could *make* Rhonda ask me to her party," Mikey said. "And put off going to Mom's until tomorrow morning." She thought about this. "Or Margalo could. Could you, Margalo? Will you? Figure out how to make Rhonda ask me?"

Margalo was gathering her books because the bell was about to ring. The lunch duty faculty had already left the room, and many of the students had too.

"Will you?" Mikey demanded. "Are you paying attention?"

No, Margalo wasn't, but now she started to. She thought about Mikey's request. She thought about how much Rhonda would hate having Mikey at her party, and considered ways for Mikey to get there. If, for example, Mikey just went up to Rhonda and asked, "What time should I tell my dad the party will be over?" Probably Rhonda would answer the question before she understood the implications, and that would be as good as an invitation.

It might be fun, getting Mikey to Rhonda's party.

But—"It's too late this time," Margalo realized. "Because you know how your mother is about changing her plans."

"Inflexible," Mikey agreed. "I know what you mean. It makes her really hard to deal with," Mikey acknowledged, then demanded, "What are you all laughing at?"

# 6
# TELEPHONE MADNESS

All that week Mikey had tried to get Shawn's phone number. What was wrong with calling him up, anyway? If she was the boy, and he was the girl he (really she) wanted for a girlfriend, it would be a perfectly OK thing for him (really her) to call her (meaning Shawn).

For the first couple of days she'd tried just asking him. "Hey, you know? I don't know your phone number," she said in the hall between classes, and "That's right," he said. Next time she was more direct. "What's your phone number?" He didn't answer, just went on talking to whoever he was talking to at lunch, some preppy in a little short skirt and a little short sweater. He ignored Mikey.

Or at least he *tried* to ignore her. "Yeah, but what is it?" Mikey asked. She figured out later that maybe she should have waited until he was alone; but since he was never alone, what was the point?

"Why do you want my number?" he asked.

"If I want to call you up. So what is it?"

"Umm," he said. And then, "It's unlisted." And then, "My parents don't want me giving it out." Until finally she figured out that he didn't want to tell her.

And *that* was sort of embarrassing. But she refused to be discouraged. He just needed to get to know her better.

And she finally did find out his phone number. There weren't that many Macavitys in the phone book, so what she did was: Call each one until some man said, "Shawn's out. Who's this?"

Mikey hung up. Fast.

It was almost a relief to be at her mother's for the weekend. It was a breathing space, like the changeover time in a tennis match, when you can sit down and gather your resources, think, get back in gear so when you return to the court you can blast through whatever defenses the opposition tries against you. Mikey was ready for a little time-out, to focus her mind and formulate a game plan. Despite her mother's hot news item, that was what Mikey did.

As soon as she got home on Sunday afternoon, Mikey planned to telephone Shawn. But her father wanted to talk. Luckily, he didn't want to tell her much about the two dates he'd gone out on that weekend—to a movie on Friday evening ("Do you realize that according to Hollywood, I should be dating someone *your* age?") and out to dinner on Saturday ("A bistro-style place, not as upmarket as the ones

77

your mother's dates take you to")—with two women he'd asked out but probably wouldn't see again. "I don't know, there just wasn't anything going on between us, you know?" He didn't expect Mikey to know and didn't pay attention when she nodded her head, Yes, she did know.

Equally luckily, he had to go to work. There was a project due to be completed by midweek and he'd promised to meet one of the members of his group at the office, if that was all right with Mikey?

That was fine with Mikey. She'd have the house to herself for a couple of hours. She'd have the phone to herself.

"Maybe we'll order pizza for dinner. How does that sound to you?"

It sounded fine to Mikey. She'd have full use of the kitchen, too.

Then, "Everything go OK for you in the city?" he asked.

"Yeah, sure. I'll tell you about it later."

"Because I think she's up to something," he said.

"She is. Do you want to hear about it now?" she asked, hoping he'd say no. He didn't disappoint her.

By the time the door finally closed behind her father, Mikey had used up her scant supply of patience. Then she had to wait until she got calmed down about calling Shawn up: It would be just the two of them talking—almost the same as being alone with him. She felt jittery, the way she did before a tennis match, excited. She knew that pre-match jitters upped her adrenaline level, which gave her more energy and better focus, but for a telephone call, who needed them?

Although, these jitters were more fun than the tennis ones. They had *Maybe-maybe* promises and *what-if*s. Maybe today was the day Shawn Macavity would start to like her back. What if he asked if he could come over? Should she ask him to stay for dinner? What were they having for dinner? Not pizza, if Shawn was coming. If Shawn was coming for dinner she wanted to cook something really good. If the way to a man's heart was through his stomach.

But first she was going to have to call him up. *Get* to call him up.

There was no question whether or not Mikey remembered the number. The second she knew which Macavity it was, that number was memorized. So she sat down at the desk in their living room and took a diaphragm-deep breath, letting the air out slowly as she counted to twelve. Then she picked up the phone and punched in Shawn's number.

It rang once, twice, three—

"Hello?" he said.

Mikey swallowed and couldn't find any words in her head. She couldn't reach any words to pull up out of her throat. *Sewage!* she thought.

"Hello? . . . Hello?"

Mikey held the phone up against her ear and did not say one word. She wet her lips, trying to speak. *What's wrong with you?* she demanded.

"Who *is* this?"

When she didn't answer, he hung up.

Mikey listened to the dial tone, then held the phone out in front of her and glared at it. "Sewage and garbage," she muttered. *Now* she could speak. "S! and G!" Furious, she tried again.

She chose not to punch redial, because she liked touching the digits of his telephone number, one after the other, like saying the letters of his name.

"Hello!" he said, the voice of someone expecting trouble.

"Shawn?"

"Yeah, why?"

"You might have a brother."

"So what if I do? What do you want?"

She thought fast. "Are you taking seminar?"

"No. Why?"

"Just because. I just—just because—I just wondered if you were," she said. She knew how dumb she sounded, but she was so busy hearing his voice—talking just to her, just the two of them—that she couldn't remember to say what she'd called him about.

"Well, now you know," he said. "Who *is* this?"

She hung up.

Mikey got up from the desk and went out to the kitchen. She opened the refrigerator door and looked inside. She closed the refrigerator door. She took down a jar of peanut butter and a box of Ritz crackers but then didn't want those, either, so she put them back into the cupboard. Then she slammed her hand down—*hard*—slamming the palm flat against the countertop, and went back to the desk.

This time she did punch redial. Enough fooling around.

"Hello," he announced, the voice of someone who really wished his phone hadn't rung.

"I meant to say, before, I've been thinking about what you said."

"Hunh?"

"About how stupid it is to get into fights."

"Is this Mikey?"

"And I think you're right. Except in self-defense, of course—but in general, I've decided I'm not going to fight. I wanted to tell you that."

"Oh. Well. OK. Good-bye."

He hung up.

Before she had to think anything about that conversation, Mikey punched speed dial 1. She had a sudden urge to talk to Margalo. Of course it was answered by Esther, Margalo's younger stepsister.

"Hello?" Esther said.

"I want to talk to Margalo," Mikey said.

"Hi, Mikey. How was your mother?" Esther asked.

"Is she there?" Mikey asked.

"Ladybug is going to have kittens. Did Margalo tell you?"

"Are you going to get Margalo, or what?"

"Then we're going to have her spayed. Because the shelter will do it for just five dollars, so we're going to have them all spayed."

"MARGALO!" Mikey yelled, yelling right into the phone as if she could yell loud enough for her voice to go in one of Esther's ears and out the other to where Margalo would hear it, and come out of her room or wherever she was in that crowded little house, and Mikey could tell her about the phone call to Shawn.

"Or neutered," Esther continued.

Mikey took a big breath. "That's good," she said. She smiled, as if Esther was in front of her and could see her face with its *This-is-your-last-chance-before-I-blow-up* smile and respond appropriately by running for the hills, or—much better—running for Margalo. "That's nice," Mikey said, smiling, "and I'm glad we had this little chat, Esther, but now GET MARGALO OR THE NEXT TIME I SEE YOU YOU'LL BE SORRY!"

"Are you coming over today?" Esther's voice rang with hope.

"No. Not today. Today I'm calling. On the telephone. TO TALK TO MARGALO!"

"Well, OK. OK. O-kay." Esther's voice turned away from the phone and Mikey heard her yell, "Margalo? It's for you. Hurry up, it's Mikey."

"I'm busy," was Margalo's greeting.

Mikey heard the clatter as Margalo took the phone off its place on a little table in the upstairs hall and carried it into the bathroom, shutting the door behind her for privacy.

"Mr. Schramm loaned me a book on gemstones," Margalo

said, "to understand how opals are formed." Ordinarily, Mikey would have insisted on being told about this, but today there were more important things than keeping ahead in science.

"I just called him," she said.

"Mr. Schramm?" Margalo sounded shocked.

"Shawn."

"Shawn? Why?"

"I got him a present." And she'd forgotten that entirely. That was something else she could have told him.

"Why would you do *that*, Mikey?"

"Mom's going to get married. She has a ring."

Margalo's voice was settling down for a conversation, as if she had gotten herself seated on the bathroom floor, leaning back against the door, ready to talk. "Of course she has a ring. I bet it's a diamond. Is it?"

"About twenty carats."

"Can't be. She wouldn't be able to lift twenty carats. She'd look like some monkey, dragging her hand along the floor—"

They were both laughing then.

"What *did* you call him about?" Margalo asked.

"Nothing special. Not really."

"Then why call?"

"To say I thought he was right about how fighting is stupid. And I do."

"I thought we were going to take martial arts in high school."

"That's not fighting. That's self-defense, against muggers and rapists."

"And bad dates," Margalo added. "And bad husbands. But are you expecting to *ever* go on a date? I mean, before high school."

"Do we *want* to?" Mikey answered her own question silently. No, not on a date; but if Shawn Macavity were to ask her to the movies? She'd go like a shot. Or to the dance. "Do you?"

"That's not exactly a pressing problem," Margalo said, then asked, "So after that what did you talk about?"

Mikey tried to think of something to say where she wouldn't look like as much of a numbchuck as she was afraid she'd been. "What?"

"You didn't have any plan, did you? You couldn't think of anything to say, could you?"

"So what? And she took me shopping."

Margalo always knew who Mikey was talking about, which was something Mikey really liked about her. "You let her take you shopping?"

"She gets a lot of boyfriends, if you notice."

"You go shopping for *things*, not boyfriends," Margalo pointed out.

"We went shopping for clothes, as it happens."

There was a silence. Then Margalo repeated what Mikey had said, only in a deliberately expressionless voice. "You went shopping for clothes. With Ms. Barcley."

Mikey let up on her friend. "Mostly clothes for her. For her trousseau. They think they'll live in Dallas."

"What about her job?"

"The bank has offices everywhere. All she has to do is transfer."

"Did you like him?"

"His children are grown up. One just had a baby, so he's a grandfather."

"It's not as if you have to live with them."

"He asked me how I'd like to spend Christmas in the Bahamas."

"Wow."

"I know." Mikey waited, then, "But still," she said.

"Maybe your mom always wanted to be someone's trophy wife," Margalo suggested.

"She said I should tell Dad her news."

There was another silence.

Mikey broke it to ask, "What kind of a plan would I have had? If I'd had one."

"What?"

"When I called Shawn. You accused me of not having a plan. As if you would have."

Margalo had her answer all ready. She was so ready to tell it that Mikey almost cut her off, but she decided not to. What if Margalo had some good advice?

"What you do for a telephone op is, you make a list—so you won't not have anything to talk to him about. A list of questions, because when you're talking to someone you like, you lose track of what you're thinking."

"How do you know that?" Mikey demanded. "Have you been talking to Aurora about me and Shawn?"

"You didn't tell me not to. I didn't think it was such a secret."

"Why would I want it to be a secret?" Mikey asked. "What kind of a chicken do you think I am?" Having settled that subject, she went on. "I'm going to make some cookies—do you want to hear my idea for a new recipe?"

"No," Margalo said.

*Now* what was wrong with Margalo?

"Then, good-bye," Mikey said. She didn't have time to waste trying to sweet-talk Margalo into a better mood.

She was creaming a cup of sugar into half a pound of butter when the phone rang. *Margalo*, she predicted, betting with the odds, although she knew better than to predict an apology. She had to go out to the living room to answer the phone. Although there were two bedrooms and two and a half bathrooms, their ranch-style house had only one television set, and phone. (In order to live within his after-the-divorce income, Mikey's father had moved them into a smaller house in a much less upscale neighborhood, which suited both of them.) She still would have liked to have a second phone, in the kitchen. In fact, what she really would have liked was a phone of her own again, in her bedroom, her own private line, but she'd settle for a kitchen phone.

She ran to get the phone before the answering machine

kicked in. It had to be Margalo, to finish telling Mikey what Aurora had said about Shawn.

"Did she have any ideas?" Mikey asked without even saying hello.

But it wasn't Margalo. A male voice asked, "Is this Mikey?"

Not her father, either. This voice wasn't as deep as her father's, and besides, her dad always started off, Hi honey, it's me.

"Yes," she said.

"Oh, good," he said. "Well, Mikey," he said. "So . . . how are you?"

"Who is this?" she demanded. "I'm busy making— Shawn?" she asked, although she didn't think so. It didn't sound like Shawn. This voice was richer, or heavier, than Shawn's; it sounded older.

"Not Shawn," he said. "Sorry." He didn't sound sorry, though. He sounded smiley.

"I *am* busy," she told him.

"Making cookies?" he said. She didn't answer, so after some empty airtime he asked, "Do you cook other things? Or do you only bake?"

He didn't sound like any boy she knew. He didn't sound grown up, but he also didn't sound like an eighth-grade boy. No eighth-grade boy, for example, would be interested in cooking. "What do you want?" she asked.

"What?" he asked, apparently surprised; at least, his voice gave way a little at the edges, like a stiff gate just starting to open. "I called so we can talk," he said then, his voice back to normal. If that *was* normal.

"Who are you?"

"You don't know me," he answered quickly. He'd been expecting that question.

"Then how do you know *me*? Do you play tennis?"

"No, but I've seen *you* play."

"Creepy," she said. "Why would you do that?"

"Why do you think?"

Definitely creepy, unless—Was he flirting with her? He was flirting with her! Who would flirt with *her*? "You said I don't know you, so how can I know why you do something dumb like watch me play tennis? Or call me up." A thought struck her. "Is this Louis?"

When he laughed, he sounded—just briefly, just for the time the laugh took—younger than before, the same way her father sometimes sounded like a kid when he was laughing at some movie they'd rented. "Not Louis Caselli," he said. "Scout's honor."

"Are you a Boy Scout? Who *are* you? Are you in my class?"

"I'm not your age," he said, another question he'd expected.

"Are you stalking me? Because I wouldn't try that if I were you."

His voice slipped again, as if she'd made some joke. "No. I swear, I'm—I'm just—" His voice deepened. "I'd like to talk to you, just sometimes. But talk—not E-mail or chat-room kind of conversation. I mean, voices. I mean . . . genuine talking."

"What about?" Mikey demanded.

"Anything. Whatever we want to talk about," he said, now as confident as if he was reading lines from a script, so he knew exactly what he'd say. "We could talk about Shawn. Or, the Australian Open, or who'll be your mixed doubles partner this year, or what colleges we like, or—It would be interesting for me to talk to someone like you. You're smart, and not many girls have . . . such strong personalities. You do"—but Mikey already knew that—"and Margalo, too. But not as much. Or we could talk about your goals, you know, in life. Or Shawn."

"You already said him."

"Oh." And that seemed to run him out of words.

Well, at least she had unsmoothed him a little. But only for a second or two, because he was right back suggesting, "Will you think about it? I mean, you don't have to want to—talk to me, I mean. I know most people would think this is sort of scary. I'll call you again—next Sunday?—so you'll have time to think, and you can tell me what you've decided. I mean, about talking to me."

"How will I know it's you?" She had him there and quickly put on pressure. "Well?"

"You'll know," he told her, not at all trapped. "So you'll think about it?"

"It's dumb," she said. "It's pretty weird. Not scary," she told him, in case he thought he *could* scare her.

"I'll call you next weekend," he said.

"Don't bother."

"It's no bother," he assured her.

"Right," Mikey said. "If you say so," she said. "Good-bye," she said, and hung up, getting the last word.

Then she punched speed dial 1.

"Margalo?" she asked.

"No, Mikey, it's Susannah." Another stepsister, older, this one from Margalo's stepfather's previous marriage. "You talked longer than five minutes last time," Susannah said, all highschool-junior important. "I'm expecting a call."

"OK. OK. Get Margalo, will you?"

"An important call."

"I know the rules," Mikey answered. Margalo's family—having not only two adults but also a large number of children, assorted stepsiblings and half siblings, having a lot of people in it, even subtracting the two oldest, who lived away from home—had only one phone and consequently a five-minute limit to all calls, unless it was an exception. Exceptions were possible, but only Aurora and Steven could make them.

"Mikey?"

"I just got this phone call," Mikey answered. She told Margalo what he had said and what he had sounded like—most importantly, like no one she recognized, especially not Shawn Macavity—and then she waited.

"A secret admirer?" Margalo guessed. "But that doesn't make sense."

"And you'd know about that, Miss Popularity."

"You're sure he's not a stalker?"

"He said he wasn't."

"What's he going to say? *Why, yes, thank you for asking, I am a homicidal psychopath*? I mean, Mikey," Margalo argued.

"How dumb do you think I am?" Mikey demanded.

"Since you ask? Sometimes you're not very smart."

Mikey hung up. Even if she was being stupid, which she wasn't, it wasn't very helpful of Margalo not to be more helpful about this. She returned to the kitchen, picked up her wooden spoon, and started to beat the batter. She hadn't taken more than twenty good strokes before the phone rang again. "Oh, mudpi-ye-es," she cried, dragging out the last vowels as she ran out to the living room. "What do you want?" she demanded of the telephone.

"Hi, honey, it's me. What's wrong?"

"Too many phone calls," she told him.

"Let the machine answer," he advised. "Listen, if I don't make it home for dinner, would you be all right with that?"

"Why?"

"We're thinking of stopping off for dinner on the way home. We're almost finished, but it's getting late—"

"You're having another date?"

"It's just a quick dinner," he told her. Then he asked, "Would you like to join us?"

"On a date? You've got to be kidding, Dad."

"I'll be home by eight at the latest." She knew he would be. "I could bring you a carryout," he offered. "Or there's lasagna in the freezer, and Swedish meatballs—"

91

"I know what's in our freezer, Dad," she reminded him. "I'll be fine. See you later. Have a good time—*on your date*," she said, and hung up before he could deny it again.

What was the world coming to? Here was her father, who had been socially dead for more than two years, turning into The Mad Dater. Here she was—and she didn't have any illusions about her popularity rating—with some secret admirer who knew what she'd like to talk about, if she decided she did want to talk to him. These things were not a bit normal.

She wished she could call Margalo again. Maybe she would, after she got these cookies out of the oven. She added eggs and oatmeal to the batter and mixed it together. She added whole wheat flour and white flour. She stirred in raisins, then—the crowning touch—macadamia nuts. And the phone rang again.

"I didn't mean you're stupid," Margalo said. "Just, sometimes you don't use your common sense, that's all. So what did he want to talk about?"

Mikey didn't need any formal apology, not from Margalo. Besides, she wanted to hear what Margalo had to say more than she wanted to hear any apologizing. "I told you," she answered, "he had all kinds of things we could talk about, if I wanted to."

"Did it sound like a list he'd made before he called? Because I asked Howie, and he said a list would be a real junior-high thing to do."

"Your stepbrother is not someone whose opinion on anything to do with romance I trust. Howie's the one who got arrested for loitering around some girl's house in the middle of the night, in case you remember. Unless, do you think it could be Howie?"

"I don't think Howie has a secret crush on you, if that's what you mean."

Mikey didn't say anything.

"Although, I guess if he did, I wouldn't know about it," Margalo admitted. "Otherwise it wouldn't be secret."

"I don't think he does either," Mikey admitted. "Do you think it's sunspots? Because things aren't acting normal, everything isn't."

"I don't believe in sunspots, but . . . You know, when you really like someone—"

"Like Shawn," Mikey said.

"Your feelings—because they're so strong—they make things seem different. They make everything *seem* not normal," Margalo said. "You know? Like rose-colored glasses? Love makes you wear not-normal-colored glasses."

"How would you know?" Mikey demanded. Then, when Margalo didn't say anything for a long time, she pointed out, "I never said I was in love with Shawn Macavity," so that she could have the pleasure of putting those five words together in one sentence, and say them aloud.

# WEEK TWO

## GIRL CHASES BOY

# 7
# *THE PLOT THICKENS*

On the bus to school Monday morning Margalo became aware that over the weekend something had happened. As in, Something Had Happened.

It was impossible to overhear any of the whispered conversations that occupied many of the eighth graders. They talked by twos and threes, heads close together, one person reporting, the others amazed. Margalo spent the ride in mounting curiosity, trying to think of how to find out what was up, who would know and tell. But when she glimpsed Mikey, that curiosity was driven from her mind.

Because Mikey wasn't wearing the cargo pants she had worn to school every day for the last year and a half. She was wearing normal jeans. CKs was Margalo's guess, and if not absolutely normal (they were black, not blue), more normal than usual for Mikey, for whom not at all normal was the norm. And she was wearing black tie shoes—could they be

Mephistos?—not sneakers. And who knew what she had on under her jacket after a weekend with her love-struck mother.

If Ms. Barcley *could* be love-struck, which—in Margalo's opinion—was about as likely as a teacher admitting ignorance. Although, Mrs. Brannigan was one teacher who seemed OK about not already knowing every right answer. But she'd had her husband taken from her by a younger and prettier gym teacher, so she had a good grip on reality. Mr. Schramm, too, seemed pretty much free of the usual teacher vanities and authority needs. Then Margalo remembered their fifth-grade teacher, Mrs. Chemsky, and grinned.

"What's so funny?" Mikey demanded. They were standing by the bus, letting the cold wind blow at their backs. She clutched a Chez ME bag, a brown lunch bag with the name of their cookie business stamped on it in bright white letters.

"Fifth grade was," Margalo answered, wondering about the bag. They couldn't reopen the business until after the seventh-grade bake sales were over, after the dance, so why the bag?

"Fifth grade wasn't funny," Mikey told her.

"What do you have? Cookies?"

"They're not for you," Mikey said, and started off toward the entrance. "Although," she added, "fifth grade was fun. Do you think little kids have more fun?"

Margalo stopped. She gathered her eyebrows together and then lowered them toward her pursed mouth, squeezing her features tight in concentration. She dropped her book bag on the ground, bent her head forward, made a fist out of her right hand and leaned her forehead against it. For a minute she held that pose—the famous statue, visibly thinking.

Mikey sighed loudly, and waited.

At last Margalo raised her head, lowered her fist, unsqueezed her face. "No," she said. And moved on into the school building, with Mikey beside her.

"Ha ha," Mikey said. Then, as they walked past the policeman watching over the entrance, she started in on how if you want to keep kids from shooting one another in school, you're going to have to get guns out of the hands of grown-ups. "Kids aren't the problem," Mikey said. "Grown-ups are the problem."

"Politicians are the problem," Margalo contributed.

"This is a democracy," Mikey reminded her. "Politicians are elected to office." She got the last word. "By grown-ups."

It was always refreshing to start the day with a little R&R. It put Margalo's brain on alert. At their lockers she demanded, "Show. Show me what you're wearing."

Mikey offered her a cookie instead. "Try this." Then, without unzipping her jacket, she unpacked weekend homework books and papers into her locker, reserving those she would need for the first two periods.

Margalo persisted. "I've noticed the jeans, and that you're wearing shoes."

"I always wear shoes," Mikey pointed out.

Margalo wondered what exactly Mikey had hidden under the jacket. "I mean, you're not wearing sneakers."

"It's a recipe I made up," Mikey said. "Actually, it's my adaptation of a standard recipe."

Margalo took a bite and watched Mikey, waiting for the jacket to be unzipped. She chewed, swallowed, taste-tested. "Good."

"I brought some for Shawn," Mikey told her, that gleam in her eye again. She had some plan of attack, Margalo thought. The cookies were part of it and whatever was under her jacket was part of it, and there was probably more. Sometimes, Margalo didn't care how tunnel-visioned and self-involved Mikey was; she just admired her for reaching out with both hands to try to grab what she wanted. Mikey didn't play things safe. She didn't worry about what people might think, or say, she didn't get embarrassed about her own feelings, she just went after what she wanted—in this case, Shawn Macavity.

Margalo took another bite. She chewed, swallowed, and watched Mikey, waiting to see what there was to see.

Mikey couldn't delay it any longer, but she kept her back to Margalo while she took off her jacket and folded it into her locker. Then she whipped around to get whatever Margalo was going to say over with. But Margalo didn't say anything. She just looked. Then, after a good long stare, Margalo raised her hand and twirled it in the air, the forefinger raised.

Mikey wanted to pretend that she didn't understand, but she turned in a stupid circle.

Her mother had called it *cute*—almost enough to make Mikey refuse to own the thing, despite its broad vertical stripes ("So slimming," chirruped the saleslady) in rusty brown and browny orange colors that Mikey happened to like. "She has lovely skin," the saleslady had murmured to Mikey's mother. "From her father's side? She'll make a nice-looking woman when she grows up."

Mikey's mother had answered without lowering her voice, or as if Mikey wasn't there, or couldn't hear, or something. "I have no idea *what* she's going to make, except things hard on herself," she'd said, while Mikey stood there, furious because she actually wanted the thing.

Mikey rotated twice for Margalo, and still Margalo didn't say anything. So she told her about that shopping scene. "My mother said that, even after I was her perfect shopping companion, all day. Muck and mire, Margalo, I went along with everything. I don't know what she wants."

"Money," Margalo said, still absorbed in staring. "Your mother wants the things money can buy, like status and envy and fancy vacations in fancy vacation destinations. Although I have to admit, she has good taste. That's a great top."

Mikey staggered, backwards—two staggering steps—until she crashed into the wall of lockers. She patted frantically at her heart with one hand. "A compliment," she gasped. "A clothing compliment."

"Well it is," Margalo insisted. "Coming?"

Mikey shook her head. If Margalo thought the top was

101

great, probably it was, which was just what Mikey hoped for. And now she had cookies to deliver. Last Friday, after lunch, she'd given Shawn a chocolate chip cookie when he was on his way to change for gym. "Unh, thanks. It looks good," he had said and "It is," she had promised him, then hung around for a few seconds to be sure he didn't have anything else to say. Today she had six oatmeal raisin macadamia-nut cookies for him, and she hadn't set her eyes on him since Friday afternoon when she watched him step up into his bus. A weekend was about as long as she could stand without seeing Shawn Macavity's face, but she didn't say this to Margalo. To Margalo she just said, "You go ahead."

Margalo's loose-leaf notebook was crammed with papers, probably some special extra-credit science work she asked Mr. Schramm for so she could get a perfect 100 in science. She said, "You look good, Mikey."

"Who cares?" Mikey asked, before she remembered that to look good was why she was wearing these clothes and realized what a dumb thing she'd just said. But by then Margalo had moved off and Mikey's full attention returned to Shawn. She didn't have a single class with him but he was in Mrs. Brannigan's homeroom; she had found that out.

"Whoa, whazzis?" somebody—Cassie—asked from behind her. "Mikey? Is that you?"

"Who'd you think it was?"

"Somebody who cared about how she looked." Cassie fell

into step beside her. "Which is not you. That El Dente really is a miracle worker if he can change *you*."

Mikey shook her head, denying it.

Cassie just put on a *You-might-deny-it-but-I-know-better* kind of smile that—before she realized how stupid fighting was—used to make Mikey want to pop the smiler a good one. "Why should I want to change?" she demanded.

"For Shawn."

"For who?" Mikey didn't want to talk about Shawn to Cassie, who was not—as in not one bit, not at all, not in the slightest—a fan of his. In fact, Cassie was getting a reputation for how little she thought of Shawn Macavity.

"Shawn. Him with the one little brain rattling around in his pretty head. El Dente—the tooth. You know exactly who I mean and the way he's got you playing dumb is just another of his wonderful transformations of the entire female population of West Junior High into babbling idiots. Into babblinger idiots than usual, I mean."

"What do you have against him?" Mikey asked.

Cassie shrugged. "He thinks he's so great," she explained. "Just because—" She didn't finish that sentence. "I'm sick of him already and it isn't even homeroom. Gotta go. Did you two hear about Heather's party?" she asked over her shoulder. "Wait'll you hear," and she had joined up with Jace.

Mikey had someplace to get to anyway, and no time to waste. In fact, she had just wasted all the spare time she had and now she would be late to homeroom. *Too bad*, she decided, and jogged down the hall.

People got in her way from both directions as she ran. Sometimes someone noticed her, but mostly not. "Looking good," Tan said and "Where'd you get the top?" Derrie wondered. Heather McGinty took time off from her intense conversation with Rhonda Ransom to comment, "Very hot," in her pruniest voice.

Mikey didn't care about any of them, although she did notice that Rhonda looked angry, and weepy around the eyes, limp in the hair. Heather, by contrast, looked bright and shiny.

"It was a mis-*take*," Heather said to Rhonda, who didn't seem to believe her.

"I don't care," Rhonda—a bad liar—lied.

"An honest mistake," Heather said. She was a better liar than Rhonda, but not a better actress, and the little twitching of smile, a smirky smile that was dying to get out, gave her away.

"I just want to be told," Rhonda whined.

Then somebody whistled and Mikey wheeled around—but saw nobody who looked whistly—and maybe the person wasn't whistling at her, or maybe it was sarcastic whistling, and she wasn't about to care. Being whistled at made her want to go home and put on a blanket.

But not before Shawn Macavity had seen her in this new outfit.

She found Shawn at the center of a group of boys and girls, all eighth graders, standing outside his homeroom door.

Mikey's plan was to think of a question she could go into the room and ask Mrs. Brannigan about; then, on her way out of the room, she would stop by Shawn's desk to give him the cookies. That was her plan, and it was a fine plan, except that as soon as she saw Shawn her brain froze. Stopped. Stopped working and just—

She had forgotten his smile. Forgotten his long legs in their black jeans. She slowed down, even though her plan was to go right on into the homeroom.

Shawn was saying no to something Ralph was asking him; he shook his head, no, and smiled, while their audience watched them.

Mikey went slowly by—he was wearing a blue V-necked sweater over a black T-shirt; and she had remembered correctly, he did have blue, blue eyes—to enter the bright, square homeroom and head up to the teacher's desk. But Mrs. Brannigan was accepting a note from a student, and reading it; so Mikey waited by the chalkboard behind the teacher's desk. Picking up a piece of yellow chalk, she wrote Shawn's initials, SM, in tiny letters at the bottom of the green board. In front of them she wrote ME, and then she put a plus sign in between. It felt good to join their initials. She imagined Shawn seeing it, the mini parade of initials, his and hers.

By then the two voices behind her had finished their conversation. Mikey turned back to the teacher, who was seated at a big desk with her blue attendance book open in front of her.

Here was a surprise. On Friday, in seminar, Mrs.

Brannigan's hair had been turning gray, and now it wasn't. On Friday the short brown curls had had splotches of gray, giving Mrs. Brannigan's head a mottled effect, like a camouflage cap or moldy chocolate pudding. Now her whole head was brown, with red highlights. But Mrs. Brannigan was definitely not the makeover type.

What was going on with everybody? She'd better read up on sunspots, Mikey thought, and then burst out, "Mrs. Brannigan, do you think that America is like the Roman Empire? Or that the former Soviet Union was, because of the way it broke up into different countries?" This could be considered a reasonable question because in seminar they had been talking about the fall of the Roman Empire.

"What?" Mrs. Brannigan looked up. "Mikey?"

"It's not urgent," Mikey said. "Never mind."

"What are you doing here?" Mrs. Brannigan asked.

The bell rang then and Mikey asked, "Can you give me a yellow slip for homeroom?"

Without even thinking—as if her mind was entirely elsewhere—the teacher pulled a pad of yellow slips out of her drawer, filled one in, signed it, and gave it to Mikey.

"Good," Mikey said, and turned to leave.

"What *are* you doing here?" Mrs. Brannigan asked.

"Nothing," Mikey said.

When she turned to face the room, Shawn Macavity had seated himself. She had her plan, and arriving at his desk, "Hi, Shawn," she said.

106

He looked up, looked right at her. When their eyes met, her heart jumped.

This was the strangest feeling she had ever had. In her whole life. The way her heart twitched in her chest. And her ribs closed around her lungs, and she couldn't think of anything to say. Wordlessly, she passed Shawn the Chez ME bag. Wordlessly, he took it.

But she hadn't turned entirely into a bowl of mush. Seeing a paper sticking out of his science book she asked, "Is that your earth science homework?"

She focused her attention on what she could see of the penciled words, the letters nothing special, pretty scrawly, a normal boy's handwriting. She would know that handwriting anywhere now.

"Yeah," Shawn answered her. "Schramm always gives big weekend assignments. I only do what I feel like."

"Me, too," Mikey said.

He waited. When she didn't leave, he asked, "Are these more cookies?"

Mikey nodded.

"Thanks," he said. "It's Mikey, isn't it?"

Mikey nodded.

Then Shawn leaned behind her, across the aisle to say something to Jason about, "I've got rehearsals after school three days a week, can you believe it?" as if Mikey had already left.

So she left.

———

What with the disproportionate time required by classes, all that time when you couldn't talk, it took Margalo most of the morning to collect information on the weekend's major developments. She learned that Ronnie's boyfriend, Doug, had been her date for Rhonda's party on Friday and brought along a couple of his high school friends. Cassie had been flirting with one of these, which made Jace jealous enough to dance with Melissa Martinez too many times—that is, enough times to look like there might be a breakup in the offing. Aimi Hearn had gone for a long walk with the other one—a talk-walk, she said, but people suspected there was more to it. Not that anyone thought she'd *done* anything, just . . . people had heard him saying he'd call her, but didn't she already have one boyfriend somewhere? Was she going to try having two? *And* the lead in the play? Some people had noticed that Ronnie didn't seem overly friendly to Doug at Rhonda's, and she looked like she was having a better time at Heather's on Saturday, without him. That was what Margalo was told, that was the rumor on Monday morning. But everybody'd had more fun at Heather's, she heard. Everybody'd said it was the best party of the year—until they found out.

Margalo spent all of her free time that morning gathering and sifting gossip, so that by the time she and Mikey entered the cafeteria for lunch, Margalo knew not only about Heather McGinty's trick—the really big story of the weekend—but also about a lot of minor eruptions of excitement, like the way Cassie did a flamenco dance whenever Shawn came near her, calling out, "Olé! It's El Dente!" and how Casey tried to make her stop but, of course, couldn't, and how Frannie—when she found out that Heather's parents weren't staying home to chaperone the party—called her father to come get her, which only Frannie could do without being a social outcast forever.

When they were seated at their usual table, and Mikey had picked up her limp grilled cheese sandwich, Margalo asked, "Did you hear about Heather's party?"

A headshake. Mikey's attention was on where Shawn Macavity stood in the lunch line.

"About what Heather did?"

Another headshake. Mikey didn't care what Heather McGinty did.

"You didn't hear about Shawn and Heather?"

"What?" Mikey demanded, turning to glare at Margalo. "What happened? Why didn't you tell me?"

Margalo took a bite of bologna sandwich, with cheese and lettuce and tomato added for flavor and nutrition. She chewed and smiled, enjoying her moment, dragging it out.

But Tan ruined it. She set her tray down on the table, sank into a chair, and asked Mikey, "So how do you feel about Heather and Shawn?"

"Heather and Shawn? What *happened*?" Mikey suggested the worst thing she could think of: "He hasn't asked her to the dance, has he?" Then she thought of something worse than worst: "She's his girlfriend? Oh, sludge," she said. "I knew I should have stayed home and crashed the party."

"You mean you haven't heard?" Tan asked. "Margalo hasn't told you?"

"*Somebody* better tell me," Mikey warned them.

Margalo let Tan do it. "Heather says it was a mistake," Tan reported, "but I don't know one single soul who believes her. Everybody knows that Heather told Shawn—when she invited him to her party—that it was going to be over a half hour later than she told everybody else. So he wasn't picked up until half an hour after everyone else."

"He was alone with her for half an hour?" Mikey asked.

"Yes, ma'am."

"That's not fair," Mikey protested.

"Her parents weren't there either," Margalo reported.

"That's cheating," Mikey protested.

"Heather's not as dumb as we thought," Margalo said.

"And they kissed," Tan said. "A lot."

"How do you know that?" Mikey demanded.

"She told everyone. She thinks—" Tan grinned and shook her head at the idiocy of some people. "I don't know what-all she thinks. Rhonda's furious, and jealous. Well, everybody's jealous, but—at Rhonda's party the night before—on Friday?—there wasn't anybody special he danced with. He danced with at least half of the girls, all the popular ones, Aimi and Rhonda, Melissa, Heather Thomas . . . all of them. Except Ronnie, of course. Slow dances, too, never the same girl twice, so everybody thought he didn't have a girlfriend.

Then today, Heather's talking as if he's hers. But"—and Tan leaned forward to tell Mikey the best bad news of all, before she started in on her lunch—"I happen to know he didn't ask her to the dance."

"Never mind the dance," Margalo said. "What does Shawn say? Has anybody asked him?"

"Yeah," Mikey echoed. "Did he say why he kissed her?"

Margalo set Mikey straight. "Shawn's a guy," she explained. "They'll kiss anyone who shoves her mouth into their faces."

"Will they?" Mikey asked.

Margalo said, "I wouldn't worry about the kissing, Mikey."

"I'm not worried," Mikey said. "I'm just jealous."

"Shawn says he got out of the house as soon as he could. He says he waited out front for his father to come pick him up," Tan reported.

"*Yes!*" Mikey crowed, punching the air with her fist.

Margalo wondered, "Do you believe him? But then, when he can have practically any girl he wants, why would he want Heather McGinty?"

"Yeah," Mikey agreed.

"I gather you've all heard the news." Cassie approached the table and pulled out a chair. "I, for one, am mightily shocked," she said, sitting down. "Ha-ha," she said. "Joke," she explained. She leaned her chair back on two legs and grinned at them with lips painted so dark a red they looked black.

111

Margalo grinned right back, noncommittal; they were two cool dudes eye-balling each other. "What *I* want is a first-hand report on *your* scene with Shawn."

"But you hate him, why would you even talk to him?" Mikey asked Cassie.

"I just wound him up a little, is all," Cassie assured Mikey.

"Where was this? When?" Mikey demanded. She leaned forward.

Cassie leaned her chair back even farther. "At Heather's. Saturday. It wasn't anything, it was"—she grinned more broadly—"fun. Actually. Poor little El Dente. He was telling someone—one of his groupies, or six of them actually, or maybe it was a dozen—he was telling them about how he's going to be an actor. You know—all the world's a stage, that whole crock? How could I pass up that opening?" Cassie asked. "I told him he looked more like a model than an actor. So he tried to figure out if that was an insult or a compliment." She rotated a fore-finger on either side of her head, "Whirra-whirra-whirra. It took a while. Right? So I told him, I meant like those models you see when you go for a haircut, in the beauty shop photo books. And he got insulted. I guess he's the *sen*-sitive type."

Margalo could pretty much picture it, the dim lighting, the loud music, people heading out the back door for privacy, in the rooms people coming and going and dancing, devouring chips and cookies and sodas. Shawn and Cassie would have been practically yelling at each other.

"So I guess he decided to get even." Now Cassie lowered

her chair, leaning toward Mikey and the rest of her audience. "So here's his idea of an insult. *I guess you weren't going in for a makeover.* Yuk-yuk, right? So I said, *What? I can't hear you,* and he tried again, *If you were in for a makeover, you were robbed.* So I said, *What? What takeover? Is there a war?* He just waved his hands and gave up. Poor guy, he just doesn't know. So I tried to give him some advice. *Tooth,* I said, *don't even try to keep up with me.* And that was that. End of scene. Except that later he tried to get me to dance with him. A slow dance. I ask you," Cassie told them. She rolled her eyes, grinned, shook her head at the hopelessness of it.

Mikey got right to the point. "Did you?"

Cassie's grin widened, and she ran her fingers through her short hair, then shrugged. "I felt sorry for the guy."

This was not the answer Mikey wanted to hear. But she persisted, "What was it like?"

"What's it ever like, slow dancing with a guy?" Cassie asked, pretending to try to remember this occasion, or—as Margalo guessed, with sudden insight—pretending to pretend, so that she could remember it all again.

"I don't know," Mikey pointed out. "That's why I'm asking."

Ronnie came to join them and say, "Asking what, Mikey? What about? The parties, right? Because of you know who. They were pretty good parties, I can tell you that—especially Heather's, well, except. I don't know what Heather was thinking." Ronnie was too shocked and nice to say more.

"What does Heather Mac *ever* think of?" Cassie asked, and answered her own question, "Boys. And how she looks."

Margalo was wondering why all of a sudden popular Ronnie was coming to sit at their table during lunch. They'd always gotten along OK with Ronnie, but not lunch-at-the-same-table OK.

Frannie and Heather Thomas sat down with them, and Doucelle, too, whom they'd known since sixth grade, with Casey tagging behind Frannie. Heather and Frannie had a question about play rehearsals. Doucelle pulled out a chair beside Tan. The rehearsal question—"Where are they held?"—and Doucelle's quiet "Wanna ask you something" to Tan did not alter the main direction of the conversation. They were girls; they could talk about seven things simultaneously, or at least three.

"It's always about looks, with boys," Cassie said.

"Ralph doesn't care that much about them," Heather Thomas announced.

"What makes you so sure?" Cassie demanded.

"Because I'm not so pretty," she told them.

They didn't agree: "You're kidding." "Who told you that?" "You've got nice hair, a good figure, your nose is . . . a great nose." "Yes, you are."

"I'm *not*," Heather insisted.

"You know?" Tan said. "My mother's boyfriend is always making these cracks—like he tells her if looks mattered he wouldn't be hanging around her."

"Your mother's *great* looking," Mikey said.

"Gets him in hot water, every time," Tan said. "She tells him, he's no prize. But they've been together for two years now. More than two years, since the summer before sixth grade, remember?"

"So there's hope for us? Just, we have to wait until we're grown up? Or until they are?" Doucelle said, laughing.

"Except for Ronnie," Margalo said. She hadn't been enjoying the look on Ronnie's face. It was the kind of look that made her want to scrub it off with a Brillo pad.

Ronnie made a bid for their sympathy. "It's not all pure fun, I can tell you. You all think I have it so easy, but it's not— I mean, I have my doubts about Doug sometimes." She looked around at them, trusting them, deciding to confide. "I mean—*doubts.*"

This was news, much more interesting than what Heather McGinty had gotten up to, and it was more current, a fast-breaking story.

"What do you mean, Ronnie?"

"What's he done?"

"He hasn't done anything wrong exactly, it's just that he's—" Ronnie made herself say it. "He's kind of jealous. I mean, why shouldn't I go to a party, even if I can't go with him?" she asked them. "It's not as if he didn't know I'm in eighth grade," she told them, pointing out a further unreasonableness. "He knew my parents won't let me go out with anyone more than once a weekend. I *told* him," she told them. "He knew all along. But now"—she leaned forward and lowered her voice—"he doesn't want me to dance with anyone but him."

"Is he that good a dancer?" Margalo asked, to keep things sane; but she was overruled.

"Uh-oh," Cassie said forebodingly.

"Possessive," Tan agreed.

"Are you going to break up with him?" Heather asked.

"He's not that great a kisser," Ronnie admitted.

They took this in, silent.

Mikey said, "I thought you really liked him. You said you did," she reminded Ronnie.

"I know what I said."

"But it's only been a month," Mikey pointed out.

"Longer—since Christmas. I don't expect you to understand," Ronnie told Mikey sadly. "Or sympathize."

"I don't," Mikey said, and left the table.

They watched her charge off, and Ronnie remarked, "I don't know why she should be so angry about me and Doug."

In Margalo's opinion, Mikey wasn't angry. She just had something else she wanted to do. Given Mikey's tunnel-vision way of life, Margalo could guess who the something else probably had to do with.

Ronnie leaned forward to speak in a low voice. "I didn't want to say this while Mikey was here, because we all know how she is." They nodded; they all knew. "But the one Doug's mostly jealous of is Shawn. And he doesn't even know him. Doug's got a brother in seventh grade, so he heard about the play and the assembly. All the attention Shawn's been getting. He's so suspicious—I mean Doug is. He doesn't trust me. I trust *him*," Ronnie pointed out. "I never worry about him with all those high school sophisticated girls. I even asked him, because he was doing nothing but arguing with everything I said, did he want to see other people? And the first thing he did was accuse me of wanting to date Shawn." That was the end of her case, and she waited—worried but hopeful—for their reactions.

"Was he always jealous?"

"I used to like it," Ronnie admitted.

"You know, jealousy can be dangerous," Tan said.

"That's just on TV," Cassie told them.

"That's not true," Casey said. They were all a little surprised to hear Casey disagree, and their surprise gave her time to express her thought before they went back to ignoring her. "In *Rebecca*," she argued. "And in *Othello*," she added. "People can die because other people are jealous."

Tan agreed. "Although, in real life they mostly get beat up. Like those women who have restraining orders to protect them from rejected boyfriends but still get beat up. Or shot. I saw it on *20/20*."

"My point exactly," Cassie said.

"Do you think Doug will beat Shawn up?" Ronnie asked, alarmed.

"More likely, he'd beat up on you," Cassie consoled her.

"You all think he's a bad boyfriend, don't you? You're not

117

saying so, and I appreciate that, but—Thanks for the good advice, guys. Doug's going to be in trouble with me when he comes over this evening."

"On a school night?"

She explained, "He comes over Mondays, after practice. Wish me luck?"

"Luck," they said.

"He's going to be surprised," Ronnie promised them. "He thinks because he's older and has a car, he rules. But I'm not about to *be* ruled."

"You go, girl," they urged her. "Go get him."

"She's already got him," Margalo pointed out. "I thought that was the problem." But only Frannie thought that was funny.

## 8
## BATHROOM TALK

What does it mean?" they asked Ronnie on Tuesday when she had gathered them in the bathroom, five of them, plus Ronnie, clustering together between the line of sinks and the line of stalls.

"Just what it looks like," Ronnie said. She leaned back against a sink, in jeans and the too-large team jacket she had worn to school. She radiated happiness and popularity, fiddling with the zipper.

Junior high didn't have team jackets. Junior-high boys weren't so tall that if they'd had team jackets, and given them to their girlfriends, the jackets would have hung almost down to the girls' knees.

"Are you engaged or something?" Tan asked.

Ronnie giggled at that suggestion. "My parents would never let me get engaged, at my age."

"So what *does* it mean?" Tan persisted.

"It means we're a couple," Ronnie told them. "I'm so *happy*," she confided. "I've never *been* so happy."

"But I thought you already were, a couple?" Derrie said.

"This means we've agreed not to see other people. Like, on dates."

"But your parents only let you go out on one date a weekend," Margalo reminded Ronnie.

"So that'll always be with Doug," Ronnie explained.

"What about parties?" Cassie wondered.

"I don't go with a date. Unless it's Doug," Ronnie said. "I'd already asked him to the dance." That memory made her smile even more happily.

Margalo had some information about coupledom from her older stepsiblings. Susannah had been half of a couple about a hundred times already, since she was always falling for someone and then discovering he wasn't perfect. Howard *wanted* a steady girlfriend. He dreamed about it, he said; it was the next best thing to getting married, he said. But Susannah and Howie never filled her in on the details—how you talked about it, what it actually required of each person. "Did *you* really ask *him* to the dance?" Margalo asked Ronnie. "Like say, *Will you go to the dance with me?*"

"Sort of." Ronnie's smile had changed to half-mischief and half-smug. "Of course, he already knew about it because of his brother. He wanted to take me—my first big dance. He made a big deal out of that, my first big dance. So when he said he hoped I was planning on asking him, I said I was. But that was way back, that was New Year's."

*Not way back*, Margalo corrected silently, then corrected herself. Maybe time did feel different to Ronnie: before Doug and after, BD and AD. Love took different people different ways; she had noticed that more than once, more than twice, too. She was glad it hadn't taken her the way it had taken Mikey.

"But you were already dating by then, weren't you? Did you know it was serious by then?" Margalo asked next.

Ronnie's mouth kept that same half-and-half smile as she remembered. "Our first date was December twenty-seventh because I met him Christmas Day and he called the day after to ask me out. And I didn't sleep barely at all that night. I *couldn't*. I kept *thinking* about him, you know? Remembering everything, every minute, every word. I was . . . in a daze, a total daze. He asked me to a movie, but"—she giggled—"we never went, we . . . just talked and stuff. So last Saturday was our five-week anniversary. He said, on our first date?, that I was his Christmas present." She smiled again. "He can be so sweet. You know? Romantic. I don't know *what* he'll do for the dance, because it's Valentine's Day."

"The jacket's an anniversary present?" Tan asked.

Annaliese said, "Aren't we too young for anniversaries? I mean, my grandparents have them. My parents would, if they were still married." She looked around for confirmation of her implied doubts.

"Doug likes to think of me wearing it," Ronnie explained. "He said. Besides, he likes to celebrate things, like, anniversaries. He likes to make things special."

"Do you do everything he likes to?" Margalo asked, and then—as the girls squealed, "Mar-ga-lo!"—realized what she might be understood to be asking, although she hadn't even thought of that until all those squeals started chasing her words around the room like some herd of baby pigs going after their dinner. "I mean—I didn't mean—"

"Margalo!" Ronnie was protesting at the same time, so their voices overlapped. Ronnie's cheeks were pink and she was loving this conversation.

So Margalo pretended she had meant what they thought she had. "Does that mean—what does Doug—I mean, for example, was there serious kissing on that first date?"

"Doug's in high school," Ronnie explained, and then searched for a way to turn the conversation in another direction. "He's a junior in high school. Only little kids think—I mean, what do you think Heather and Shawn did?"

"What do you mean?" Margalo asked. "What *did* they do?" Another round of squealing. "How do you know what they did?"

"If you must ask, Shawn told me about it. We were talking. Because—you know—when you've got a boyfriend you can be regular friends with other boys. Because everybody can relax." They made a semicircle around her, all of them reflected in the mirrors, their faces and the back of Ronnie's head, the dark fall of her hair. Nobody else came in, enabling them to continue this private conversation.

"Shawn wanted to talk to a girl about it," Ronnie said. While she thought about what more she wanted to tell them, Ronnie turned to face the mirror. She combed her hair with her fingers. "We're pretty good friends, me and Shawn," Ronnie told the girls surrounding her. "I guess I'm lucky the way I get along with boys. Except," she added, to remind them that she didn't have an entirely perfect life, "there's always Louis. Although, I did get him to stop calling Shawn names."

"That was you?" Derrie asked. "But, I thought, Shawn asked him?"

"Not that Shawn really minded," Ronnie told them. "But you know what? Doug's really jealous of Shawn. I mean—unreasonably, you know?" This pleased her. "I wish he'd understand how a girl can have close friends that are boys."

"Is that why he wants you wearing his jacket? Because he's jealous?" Margalo asked.

This, however, was a cause-and-effect question: *What is the cause of this effect?* If Ronnie hadn't been busy adding, "I don't know why he picks on Shawn," and if two groups of eighth-grade girls—a few jockettes, a couple of Barbies—hadn't entered, Margalo might have been cold-shouldered out of the room.

But Ronnie did want to exclaim over Doug's suspicions, and flaunt them, and cuddle up with them, and then the two groups did come noisily in, so Margalo escaped the consequences of motivation analysis. Everybody greeted everybody and shifted around to share mirror space, while some girls entered the stalls. Ronnie leaned over the sink to inspect her eye shadow and lipstick, to smile at herself, before she turned eagerly around to respond to the new round of eager questions. "Ronnie? Is that—? What does it mean, I mean, that jacket?"

# 9
# YOU'RE NOT SICK, YOU'RE JUST IN LURVE

H ow *could* you?" That was what Mikey wanted to ask Shawn all day Monday, and again on Tuesday—"How could you *do* that?"—when she was giving him a Chez ME bag holding chewy ginger cookies. "How *could* you kiss Heather McGinty that way?" she thought whenever she saw his face, "How could you *want* to do that?"

She didn't ask out loud, of course. Their conversations were few and brief: "I made these." "Thank you." Few and brief and not exactly brilliant was what their conversations were, with no space for questions like "How *could* you?"

She did leave messages at the bottoms of the chalkboards in all his classes, four little letters and the plus sign; no hearts, no arrows, just a little letterly reminder, in case he wanted to think about it. ME + SM. She hoped that it wouldn't be much longer before he did think about it. She hadn't been thinking about much of anything else for eight days already.

Heather was having another party on the weekend—of course. Shawn was going—How *could* he? But Mikey wouldn't have been able to go even if she had been invited. She had to go to her mother's again, a command performance. "It's our last time alone," her mother had said, "and I need you to help me pack." So while Mikey had to be back in the city doing whatever was so important to her mother, Shawn was going to a party at Heather's—*again*.

By Wednesday it was settled who was giving parties on which day, Heather on Friday and Ronnie on Saturday. Everyone—meaning primarily Shawn Macavity—would be there. But not Mikey. Not Margalo, either, which meant at least that Mikey wasn't the only person left out, but also that Mikey had nobody there who would report back to her on Sunday about what had happened at the parties. There were only ten days until the dance, and everybody knew it. If you were going to go with a date, you were running out of time to ask, or be asked.

Mikey and Margalo were having lunch together on Wednesday and talking about who already had a date, who wanted to ask who, who hoped who wouldn't ask her, and what groups were gathering to go to the dance dateless. Margalo reported, "Louis asked Frannie. Big surprise. But she said she didn't want to go with a date. So he asked Heather Mac. Then Derrie. Cheryl. Sandy. Annaliese. Then Frannie again—I think he was hoping she'd feel so sorry for him she'd say yes. But that's everybody he's asked so far. Do you think he'll ask us? I almost hope he does," she laughed. "But probably not. Probably over his dead body."

For some reason Mikey needed to say to Margalo, "I really want Shawn to ask me."

"I *am* aware of that."

"Don't be so sarcastic at me. I really do. I mean, really really."

"You've really, really told me that same thing about five hundred times," unsympathetic Margalo answered.

"*I* could ask *him*."

"And I've told you about five hundred times my opinion about that."

"What makes you think you're so right? You know," Mikey admitted, "I never wanted anything so much as him."

"Why?" Margalo asked, looking right at Mikey. "No, seriously, why do you want him? For a kissing op? Mall op? Dating op?"

"Who says there has to be a reason?" Mikey demanded. "What makes you know so much about it anyway? You've never even wanted to have a boyfriend." She looked closely at Margalo, staring into her brown eyes, unexpectedly unsure. "Have you?"

And what did it mean when Margalo smiled in that way? Not a *Lucky-me* smile or a *wouldn't-you-like-to-know* one, but as if she was sitting on a tack. "There was Ira," Margalo said.

"That was just in fifth grade," Mikey said.

"How do you know?"

"And he was never your boyfriend anyway."

"You didn't say I never had one. You said I never wanted one."

"If Ira asked you to the dance, would you go?" But before Margalo could answer that question, Mikey said, "You'd look pretty funny dancing with Ira Pliotes."

"I didn't say *now*," Margalo said, with that tack-sitting smile.

And suddenly there was Ralph Cameron standing in front of her. Ralph just loomed up behind Margalo's back, with his floppy brown hair and the rugby shirt boys were wearing that winter. "What do *you* want?" Mikey demanded.

"Hey, Ralph," Margalo said, turning her head to look up at him and then looking back at Mikey with her eyebrows raised in a question.

"Hey, Margalo," Ralph answered. "Listen, Mikey, I want to ask—"

"No," Mikey said.

Margalo made a wrinkly face at her, a *What's-wrong-with-you?* face. But what was so wrong with not wanting someone to ask you to a dance when you already knew you wouldn't go with him? She'd just said her no early, that was all.

"Give me a chance," Ralph said. "I only want to ask—"

"But why, when I already said no?" Mikey demanded.

She didn't think it was particularly smart of Ralph to ask her to the dance, when everybody knew how she felt about Shawn.

"Because we'd win," Ralph said.

"Win what? Is there some contest at the dance?"

"Not the dance," Ralph said, as if that was the wildest idea he'd heard all morning, or all year. "Geez, Mikey—you didn't think . . . ? How could you think . . . ? I'm taking Heather to the dance, everybody knows that. You're really weird, Mikey."

"Oh, yeah?"

Well, maybe she was, because it was disappointment she was feeling now, finding out that Ralph didn't want to ask her to the dance.

"Yeah. You are. But I still think you'd make me a good partner in mixed doubles. For tennis. This spring. I'm talking about tennis, Mikey."

"Mixed doubles?" At least that made sense. She tried to remember what kind of a game Ralph played. "You're asking to be my mixed doubles partner for the tennis team?" Ralph wasn't a bad player, she remembered, trying to recall his service returns, if he approached the net behind them. "I'll think about it," she promised him.

"We could win big time," he told her.

"I said I'd think about it," she told him. And she would, but now she wanted him to go away, because what if Shawn saw her talking to Ralph, and thought she was fickle and had already gotten interested in somebody else, and wouldn't even consider liking her back because of that. "So—that's that," she said, and dismissed him. "What are you hanging around for?"

And now Margalo had covered her eyes with her hands and was shaking her head, *No, no, no, no, no.*

"*What?*" Mikey demanded, but before Margalo could start telling her how dumb she was, Mikey went back to what really interested her. "What days do you have rehearsals?" she asked Margalo, to which the answer was, Tuesday, Wednesday, Thursday, when usually no teams had games, so then Mikey wanted to know, "Are these rehearsals in the auditorium?" to which the answer was, "No, in Ms. Larch's classroom. Why?"

As if Margalo didn't already know.

What Margalo didn't tell Mikey—because she didn't want to have any more conversations than they already did about Shawn Macavity, and neither did she want the job of carrying messages from Mikey to Shawn—was that Ms. Larch had her working with Shawn on his lines. That was what the early rehearsals were all about, Ms. Larch told them. "Because I wasn't born yesterday. It is hard work learning lines, and not all of us—let's face it—enjoy hard work. Lieblings," she said to them all when they had gathered for their first rehearsal, "acting is the easy part. For acting, you have an audience." She waved her scarf in the direction of where an audience would have been seated if this had been a stage, and laughed knowingly. "But first, we must all do the hard work. Onward!" she urged them. "Excelsior!"

It turned out that Shawn stank at memorizing, and he also didn't seem to be doing any preparation at home. After two rehearsals Margalo knew his Act I lines better than he did— although he didn't seem to notice that. Shawn's acting ability was physical, the way he moved his body or the way he stood still. He wasn't a natural at words, however; and sometimes Margalo had to explain to him what a line meant. "You sure?" he'd say.

Margalo would try to explain the language and the joke. "When he says he travels light, it's like, a rolling stone gathers no moss."

"Oh, *Rolling Stone*. I read that sometimes," Shawn would say. "Is that why it's called that? But all this Thomas Mendip guy does is talk. He talks too much. You know? For a soldier. And you really get off on him, don't you? That's weird. You know? You're pretty weird, Margalo. Not as weird as Mikey, but—don't get me wrong, I like you fine and you're really helping me with this."

Margalo wasn't about to tell Mikey that her wanna-be boyfriend was as thick as two planks. She wished Ms. Larch would have her work with someone else, like Hadrian, who had already made up this great voice for his role, all frothy and floaty and not at all like his usual creaky one. But Margalo was stuck with Shawn Macavity.

As they came out of Ms. Larch's room at the end of Wednesday's rehearsal Cassie happened to be there, after Art

Club, and so were some of the girls who'd had basketball practice, Mikey among them. Mikey didn't have a chance at Shawn because Cassie grabbed his attention.

"Yo, Tooth!" she called. "How could you do that?"

"Do what?" Shawn asked. "Hey," he greeted some of the other girls, "hey, hi. Hey, howareya?"

"All that kissing with Heather," Cassie said.

That got his full attention.

"I mean, she's so *blonde*—and she tricked you into it and—how could you fall for that? And kiss her like she says you did?"

"Back off, Cassie," Shawn warned. "What makes it any of your business?"

Cassie stood right in front of him. "So how was it?" She meant him to be embarrassed. "On a scale of one to ten, how do you rate kissing Heather? I should tell you, she only gave you a six."

"What?" Shawn asked. "What're—"

"All right, I lie, it was a seven."

"What did I ever do to you?" Shawn looked around to ask, "What did I ever do to her?"

"Probably it's best not to say anything. You wouldn't want to kiss and tell, would you? Although, your kissing partner doesn't have any problem with that. See you around, Tooth," Cassie said, and sauntered off.

Margalo didn't mention the scene as they rode home on the late bus. Mikey sat silent beside her until finally, two stops before Margalo was going to get off, Mikey turned from the window to ask, "Why would Cassie do that? I didn't think she disliked him that much. Not like Louis."

"D'you mean like Louis dislikes him? Which is jealousy, or d'you mean like we dislike Louis, because he's such a general twit?"

"I mean her, about him," Mikey said.

"You want to hear what I think?"

"Isn't that what I just asked you?"

"Sometimes," Margalo reminded her, "you ask me but you don't mean it."

"This time I do," Mikey said.

"I think she's got a crush on him," Margalo said.

Mikey disagreed. "It's the opposite—everybody knows that."

"It's only a theory I have."

"You think Cassie's after him too?"

"It's just a guess," Margalo said. "You know, the way sometimes someone likes someone and they deny it by acting especially unfriendly," Margalo explained.

"No," Mikey said, not at all puzzled, just irritated, "I don't know."

"It's actually a way of getting someone's attention, if you think about it. A backwards way."

"But if everybody's after him, how am I ever going to get him?" Mikey moaned. "No matter what I wear." That day she had put on a blue blouse, because her mother and the

133

saleslady said (and Margalo agreed) that the color looked good with her skin.

Margalo had her own interesting thoughts to follow. "Which makes quarreling a flirtation op."

"My mother says a woman should play hard to get," Mikey told her.

"You could say that Cassie's making sure he knows she'd be hard to get," Margalo said.

"But I don't want to *play* anything," Mikey said. "I don't even think I can."

"Because if she didn't act like that, he might not notice her at all," Margalo said.

"Except sports," Mikey said. "What do you think about Ralph being my doubles—"

But they were at Margalo's stop and she rose to go down the aisle and get off the bus.

"I'll call you," Mikey yelled after her.

Margalo had to work with Shawn again the next day, Thursday, and he still didn't know his lines. That didn't bother him. Nothing bothered him, not even when she pointed out the obvious. "You didn't do any work at all on this last night."

"I was busy." Shawn's facial expression, and the way he shifted in the desk, both said, *What's your problem?*

She told him, "As an actor, you're a natural with your body. And your face."

Praise was old news by now to Shawn.

"But you do have to know your lines."

"I'm trying," he said. "You're just some perfectionist genius. Do you expect me to be able to do everything in one night?"

She could see that half of his attention was on a cluster of girls presently studying in one corner of Ms. Larch's classroom, where movie posters decorated the bulletin boards and—now that she noticed it—there was a little line of initials at the bottom of the chalkboard, ME joined with a plus sign to the initials SM. (*Oh, Mikey*, Margalo thought, and started figuring out ways to get those initials erased without anyone noticing.)

Shawn was smiling over at Heather Thomas and Rhonda Ransom, where they were rehearsing their lines in one corner of the room. He raised his eyebrows and jerked his head toward Margalo, for their benefit. They covered up their giggling mouths as if covering up a burp, to let him know they got it. He turned his attention to Aimi.

Margalo really wished Ms. Larch had assigned her to work with Hadrian and Frannie, but they, of course, didn't need any assistance to use rehearsal time well. She could even hear them, Hadrian's voice all pompous and confident now, since he was reading the mayor's lines to cue Frannie. Margalo looked at Shawn smiling at Aimi, and sighed.

Aimi didn't smile back. "She's mad at me," Shawn said to Margalo. "Aimi, I mean. Do you think?"

"Maybe she's bored with you."

"Naw," Shawn said.

At least, Margalo reminded herself, Ms. Larch hadn't asked her to work with Louis, who had started the rehearsal by going up to Melissa, in front of everybody, to ask, "Why don't *you* be my date for the dance?" and when she said no, she already had a date, she couldn't, he turned to Rhonda. "I guess it'll have to be you."

"Let's try the first scene again," Margalo said to Shawn patiently. "Give me your first line."

He wrinkled up his face to show how hard he was thinking. With his eyes on the audience across the room, he knocked at the side of his head with the flat of his hand, as if to jar words loose in there, then rapped with his knuckles on his forehead—*Anybody home?* Finally he said, "Body?" At Margalo's expression he tried again, "Soul?"

To test him, Margalo maintained her expression.

"I give up," he said. "Tell me." Then he looked over at his audience. He moved his forefinger in a circle at his temple, then pointed at Margalo. To Margalo he said, "Don't be too weird if you can help it."

"I can't help it," Margalo said. "I don't want to help it," she told him. "I don't want to help you, either," she said.

"Hey, what'd I do?" Shawn asked.

Margalo couldn't begin to tell him.

Mikey was there again at the end of rehearsal, lurking at the door, wearing an off-the-shoulder blouse that actually,

Margalo thought, looked good. Margalo hated the style, all '70s fake peasant, but Mikey's shoulders were as round as her arms, and for the first time Margalo could see why the style had been popular. Most of the day Mikey had covered her blouse with a jacket, but this was a Shawn op so she wanted to look as good as she could.

The students in Ms. Larch's room were gathering up their books now because the bell was about to ring and they had buses or mothers to meet. Louis said, "Hey everybody, look who's here. It's Cinderella. She's come for you, Shawn."

Shawn glanced over to the doorway.

"No," Louis said, "I'm wrong. It's not Cinderella, it's her pumpkin." He laughed.

Shawn laughed with him. "Not bad, Lou." He jammed his copy of the script into his jacket pocket. Melissa called over to him, asking him something, and all of the girls except Aimi and Frannie gathered around him for a couple of minutes. Shawn bobbled from one girl to the other, before he turned his back to all of them, raised his free hand over his shoulder in a wave, and exited the room. As he went through the door he took the brown bag Mikey offered, said something without looking at her, and moved off.

Mikey followed him, not trying to catch up. Margalo actually admired the way Mikey was going after Shawn—the same way she went for an overhead smash, *whap*, as hard as she could. She didn't sympathize with Mikey's choice, but she approved of her methods.

As the room emptied, Margalo also gathered together her papers and books. "Margalo," Ms. Larch said. "Can I have just the tiniest word with you?"

Margalo waited.

"How's our Shawn doing?" Ms. Larch asked. "Or perhaps I should ask, how badly is he doing? Oh, yes, I did know it. He's my calculated risk because he looks so right. He's Thomas Mendip in his bones. But how is he doing with the lines?"

"Well, he's not a quick study—"

Ms. Larch's laughter cut her off. The teacher had a deep, chesty laugh that bubbled up through her throat, the kind of laugh you want to join in with. Margalo joined in.

"But he's such a lovely-looking boy, so handsome. However, in the interest of progress it might be that I should take over the job of rehearsing him?"

Margalo said quickly, "I'm not the right person to work with Louis."

"Oh, liebling, I *do* know that. There are the others—Aimi, Rhonda and Heather, Ira and Jason. You've done better with Shawn than I dared to hope, but I suspect that now he needs to hear that he can lose the role. He needs . . . just a pinch of insecurity, a little soupçon of fear. I promise you, I know these actors," she told Margalo. "I will not let him bring down my play."

Margalo couldn't think of what she was supposed to say. "Un-hn," she said.

"And on another topic, Hadrian has offered to share your responsibilities as stage manager. Before we accept, I need to be sure his academic work won't suffer if he undertakes two positions in the play, and one of them a performance role."

Margalo could reassure her. "If Hadrian says he can do it, he probably can."

Ms. Larch studied her, intently, dramatically. Then, "May I tell you something?" she asked. She didn't wait for an answer, and Margalo didn't try to interrupt her with one. After all, can a student say to a teacher, *No, you can't tell me something*?

Ms. Larch told her, "You know, I wanted you for Jennet—well, to be absolutely truthful, it was between you and Aimi—but Mr. Schramm convinced me that you were a better choice for assistant director. Mr. Schramm thinks very highly of you, Margalo, and not only as a student. He admires you. I want to tell you, I'm glad I took his advice. He was an actor himself, did you know that?"

Margalo nodded, unable to speak.

"I always seek out his input on my productions. So you can thank him for your chance to work with me."

Margalo nodded again.

"And you're learning a great deal, too, about the theater," Ms. Larch told her, adding one of those pronouncements teachers like to make about students, "although you don't know it."

And how she knew *that*, Margalo couldn't have said, since

it was false anyway. But she smiled and bobbed her head and was in fact quite pleased with this conversation.

It wasn't Mikey's turn for the window seat, but she got there first so she took it. All the windows in the bus were opened from the top to freshen the air inside which stank of the sweat worked up in basketball practices, especially the smell of boys' sweaty sneakers. Mikey huddled inside her jacket, trying to stay warm. This dressing to look good often meant you weren't comfortable, and she looked out the window, thinking about how cold she was. Then she turned to glare at Margalo. "You should go into business designing clothes."

She could see that Margalo had been thinking about something else. Something that made her happy, and Mikey had no idea what it might be. She thought about asking what the good news was.

Instead, "You should design comfortable clothes," Mikey said. "Comfortable *and* good looking." Sometimes she wished she could be more like Margalo, and not just to be thin. Mikey would have liked to be able to forget what Louis Caselli had said, one of his garbagy fat jokes. Or at least she'd like to be able to keep to herself how those cracks of his got through to her. Or maybe she'd just like to still be the kind of person who would pop him one on his big mouth. She heard herself telling Margalo, "I *can* diet, you know. If I want to. Even if the doctor said—I told you, didn't I?—she says I'm the middle of the upper third of the weight curve for my height."

"That's just Louis being a jerk," Margalo told her.

Mikey knew that. "I tried going on a diet," she said. "Last week. I didn't eat anything all day."

"That's not a diet, that's a hunger strike," Margalo said.

The bus jerked to a stop, let some people out, closed its doors and jerked going again.

"There's a difference between dieting and starving, and why would you do that, anyway?" Margalo asked. "What's wrong with the way you look?"

Mikey's opinion exactly. She just wanted corroboration. That settled, she asked, "So, what's got you so happy?"

"Oh," Margalo said. "Nothing," she said. "Just things," she said. "A good rehearsal. I like being assistant director, it's interesting. You know who's really good? Hadrian Klenk. He's got a terrific voice; he can sound like *anybody*. And Aimi's good too, Aimi's going to be good in that part."

"You're a behind-the-scenes person," Mikey announced. "I'm the center-stage kind."

"I noticed," Margalo said. She gathered her book bag onto her lap as they approached her stop. "She's not as good as I would have been, though," she said, getting the subject of conversation back to herself, Mikey noticed.

Well, Mikey admitted, she was pretty self-centered herself, and she thought most people were. In her experience. Only, being Margalo's friend meant that Margalo included Mikey in her self-center a lot of the time. That's what being friends was, wasn't it?

And, Mikey thought, thinking on, that's what love was too, only more so. "You know what gets me?" she asked Margalo.

Margalo was rising up, holding on to the back of the seat in front of her for balance as the bus lurched. "Everything," she answered.

"No, besides that. What gets me is the way—I mean, I know I'm not in love. Not *love*," Mikey said. "But what is the word for what I'm in? There isn't one," she told Margalo.

"Crush," Margalo suggested. "Infatuation. Puppy love."

"Those are such put-downs. What kind of a word is *crush*, for a feeling?"

"Lust?" Margalo suggested.

"Doesn't that have to mean sex? I mean, real sex," Mikey asked. She switched back to her own thoughts. "And then, I love lasagna."

Margalo was walking away now, so Mikey said to her back, "Call me. I'll call you."

Later that evening, when the phone rang, Mikey answered it cautiously. "Hello?" She didn't know, these days, who might be on the other end of the line.

"Lurve," Margalo said. "We'll call it lurve. Spelled with a *u-r*. Think about it, Mikey. You're in lurve—like a combination of lurch and love."

142

Mikey didn't waste time thinking. She tried the word on, as if it was some dress in a department store. "I'm in lurve with Shawn Macavity," she said.

"You certainly are," Margalo agreed.

# 10

## WHO SAYS *IT'S BETTER* TO GIVE THAN TO RECEIVE? WHO SAYS *IT'S BETTER* TO HAVE LOVED AND LOST?

Friday morning Mikey bolted out of homeroom two minutes before the bell rang, looking—she hoped—as if she had some bathroom emergency, and zipped down the nearly empty hallways, lickety-split, splickety-lit, to station herself outside of the door to Mrs. Brannigan's classroom. Through the glass top of the door she could see the homeroom breaking up into groups, people getting themselves out of their desks, turning to pick up their books or backpacks, talking, waiting out the last seconds before the bell. Mikey watched Shawn talking to a couple of boys, while Heather McGinty and a couple of other girls waited nearby. Shawn wore his usual black jeans and boots, this time with a loose Hawaiian shirt, all tropical flowers and bright birds on a red background. Nobody but Shawn would dare to wear a shirt like that.

Finally, the bell rang.

Mikey waited where he'd have to go past her, keeping her

eye on him as if he was a tennis ball about to come off the racquet of a good server. She heard someone say, "Hey, Mikey," and answered, "Hey, see you," but she didn't take her eyes off of Shawn.

He might get right past her if she didn't stay focused. If she let herself get distracted, he might move to where she couldn't get a good shot at him.

As soon as he stepped into the hall, Shawn was surrounded, but Mikey ignored his companions. Shawn was the one she blocked. "Hey, Shawn," she said, planted right in front of him.

"It's Mikey, right?"

"You know who I am," she told him. "I want to talk to you."

"I have to—"

"Just for a couple of minutes. You won't be late for class," she promised him. "You go ahead," she told the girls, smiling. *Don't even think about it*, her smile said, and they obeyed, reluctantly, looking back to Shawn as though if he just said the word, they would return to rescue him.

"Listen," Shawn said. He had his hands jammed into his back pockets.

Mikey reminded him, "I tried to tell you last night on the phone."

"I had homework. I couldn't talk."

Mikey looked up, keeping eye contact. "I got this for you," she said, and thrust the bag at him. "Here."

He was too surprised not to free his hands and take the bag from her. "Urban Outfitters," he commented with that lift to the voice that says, without saying the word, *Cool.*

She was waiting for him to see the shirt. "Open it," she urged.

"But it's not my birthday," he told her.

"Open it."

"Why should you get me something?"

"Just look. You'll see." She jammed her own hands into her own rear pockets and watched his face.

As he opened the bag his face looked puzzled. As he pulled out the black fabric his face looked nervous. "You shouldn't ha—," he was starting to say as he unrolled the T-shirt, held it out in front of him, read what it said. Then his face looked maybe angry, or maybe alarmed; Mikey couldn't be sure.

She reassured him. "It wasn't expensive."

"What *is* this?"

"I got one for myself, too. Mine's white." She had told her mother that this black one was a present for Margalo and had to be a medium because Margalo was so tall, even if the shirt turned out to be a little broad across the chest. "Do you think it'll fit?"

"Listen," Shawn said. "Mikey," he said. He was rolling the shirt up and returning it to the bag. "I don't want this." He held the bag out to her.

She didn't take it. "Why not?"

"That's a joke, right?" he asked, then shook his head at her.

"It's not a joke, is it? You're too weird," he said. He pulled the shirt out again and held it open in front of her—as if she hadn't already seen it.

Mikey liked that shirt, liked it a lot, in white or in black. I ME, it said—the *I* and the *ME* in big, fat white letters, the heart red and a little outsize. Just looking at that shirt made Mikey feel good. Her mother hadn't agreed, but "I don't see any harm in it," she'd said. "You two will wear the shirts once and you'll learn." *Learn what?* Mikey hadn't asked, since she figured she could fill in the blank without her mother's help: *Learn your lesson. Learn you can't.* But every time Mikey saw that shirt, in white or in black, she felt like laughing. Out loud. Because it made her so glad to be herself, Mikey Elsinger.

"Isn't it *great*?" she asked Shawn.

"Listen, Mikey," he said. He sounded so serious she changed the expression on her face to match. "I want to ask you . . ."

He stopped speaking.

She waited as long as she could before what she hoped was the end of his sentence burst out of her: "To the dance?"

"No!" Shawn cried. "Absolutely—Mikey!" he cried. "Don't you get it?"

"No!" she cried right back at him. "I don't get it."

"You're weird!" he cried.

"What's wrong with weird?" she demanded, finally feeling comfortable to talk with him now that they were having a normal conversation.

"Everything," he told her. "Just for once can't you listen? I'll keep it simple. One: I don't want your cookies. They're good, but I don't want you giving them to me. Two: I don't want this shirt with this—logo, your—on it. Now do you get it? Get this, too, Mikey, this is the big one. Three: I don't want you for a girlfriend," he said, then repeated the words with big spaces in between them. "I . . . won't . . . ever . . . want . . . you . . . for . . . a . . . girlfriend."

"Oh," Mikey said. "I get it." Not that she was exactly surprised. "OK." She was deflated, like an emptied balloon, squashed like a bug, but not surprised. It wasn't as if she'd totally lost her grip on reality. She *had* figured out that Shawn Macavity wasn't exactly madly in love with her. But she was sure he should be, so she hoped he would be. She tried to explain to him. "But—"

"Can't we just be friends?" he interrupted—the TV-show solution to awkward relationship situations—looking over her shoulder and down the hall. He wanted to get going, that was obvious.

Well, Mikey was ready to get going too. "Sure," she said. "You can think of me as a friend. I'd like that. But it won't change how *I* feel," she told him.

He stared at her. "And you don't think that's weird?"

"Or change what I think of those scummy girls who hang around you all the time," she told him.

"Unlike you," he said.

"That's different," she told him. "Because we're friends. You just said," she reminded him, proving her point.

He turned to walk away, and she watched him—but then he stopped and turned back to her, smiling, and that smile squeezed at her heart. "Mikey," he said, smiling. "If we're friends," he said. "Then can I ask you to do something?"

Was he going to ask her to the dance after all? Unlikely, improbable—but what else could it be?

"Sure," she said, looking right into his eyes. Looking into Shawn Macavity's eyes was like falling asleep when you were really tired, like the first bite of pizza or the follow-through of a one-handed backhand. Looking into Shawn Macavity's blue eyes, you didn't ever want to stop looking. Mikey had never met up with that feeling before in her life, and she couldn't get enough of it—even if he didn't want any of it, that didn't change how she felt. How could it? Why should it? She asked him, "What is it?"

"Don't put those initials on the chalkboards anymore. Will you? It's embarrassing," he said.

Not the dance, then.

Worse than not the dance.

"Sure, OK," she said. "No problem," she said, feeling now as if the words were blocks of wood she hacked off from her wooden brain and sent on out of her mouth to clatter on the floor.

"Great," he said, and turned away again.

He moved so fast toward the crowd of boys and girls ahead of him that he didn't even hear her joke. "Not exactly *great*."

But it probably wasn't much of a joke anyway. She wasn't feeling too jokey right now.

# 11
# TELEPHONE
# MADNESS MULTIPLIED

On that Sunday, Mikey's mother got her back home by
nine thirty.

A.M.

Actually, it was 9:21 A.M., so unexpectedly early that
Mikey's father wasn't there. Mikey let herself into the empty
house, put her duffel bag down on her bed, and called
Margalo. Esther answered on the first ring, as if she'd been
waiting by the phone.

"Esther it's me and I want to talk to Margalo," Mikey said.
"Right away."

"Hi Mikey! I missed you."

"That's great, Esther. Get Margalo."

"They're still asleep."

"It's nine thirty," Mikey protested.

"They're all in the living room."

"Why are they sleeping in the living room?"

"For the sleepover," Esther explained. "Wait . . . I hear—"

Margalo's mother got on the phone. "Mikey? It's Aurora, she'll be here in just—go get Margalo, Esther—are you at your mother's?"

"No."

"I have to—hold on a minute," Aurora said. Mikey heard her put the phone down and heard distant muffled voices. She hung up. What was Margalo doing having a sleepover and not inviting her, and not even telling her?

In about one-half minute the phone rang, but Mikey knew who it was. She listened to the message as Margalo recorded it onto the answering machine. "I know you're there. I bet you're angry. But it's not—this didn't even get planned until Friday afternoon, when you were already gone to your mother's. It just happened, we just decided on the phone Friday, it's only four of us who weren't going to Ronnie's, you weren't—"

The machine cut her off.

The phone rang again—one ring, two, three, four—and then the machine picked up: "We're the Elsingers. Leave us a short message."

"Mikey, for slime's sake." Pause. Humming of tape. "Pick up the phone." Pause. Humming of tape. "Come *on*, Mikey—" Cut off.

Again: "Don't be a total hairball, Mikey. Pick up the phone, I know you're listening." Pause. Tape humming. "I don't know why you think I don't know you're there. I bet I even know where you're standing. And what you're wear—"

*Ring, ring, ring, ring.* "We're the Elsingers. Leave us a short message."

"OK, Mikey. I have a baby-sitting job this afternoon, until late. So call me back or don't, it's up to you. If you'd rather be angry at me, even though there's no reason, go right ahead."

*Click. Beep.* End of message.

Best friends since the first day of fifth grade? Ha! Topsoil! Margalo knew Ms. Barcley's phone number. She could have called and—

And what? And Mikey would have known she was missing the sleepover. Was it worse to miss it and know it, or miss it and not know it?

Never mind that. Mikey needed to get angry—it felt pretty good, in fact—at somebody, anybody. And it felt better to *be* angry—and besides, Margalo knew Mikey well enough to know that Mikey would have wanted to know about it even if she couldn't go. (Just like Mikey knew Margalo well enough to know that Margalo would have included her in the sleep-over.) Mikey went out to the kitchen and poured a bowl of Cap'n Crunches, and poured milk over the crisp miniature pillows, and ate standing up. The milk-and-sugar taste, combined with the friendly crunching sound inside her head as she chewed, made her feel like a little kid.

When the phone rang again after about fifteen or twenty minutes, she still didn't answer it. "I thought you might have figured it out, but I guess not," Margalo said. "This is slime-ing stupid, Mikey."

Mikey knew that. Sometimes she liked being stupid.

Margalo waited a full ten seconds, then hung up again.

Mikey finished her cereal, rinsed the bowl, rinsed the spoon, put them both into the dishwasher. Her father wouldn't expect her home for a couple of hours at the soonest, so she didn't expect to see him until then. And where was he, anyway? Maybe she'd call Shawn. Because they were friends, that was what he'd said. Friends called each other up and talked, just to talk, so there was no reason for her not to call him now that he said they were friends.

She dialed his number and asked the man who answered if she could speak to Shawn. The first thing that popped out of her mouth when she heard his "Hello?" was: "Where's your mother?"

"At church. Why? Who is this?"

"Because she never answers the phone. Mikey."

"Listen, Mikey, I can't talk now. I'm leaving—my dad's— I'm meeting some people at the Mall."

"Oh. Oh, OK. Maybe—"

"Bye."

Mikey held on to the phone for a minute, then set it down. If that was the way everybody was going to be, she'd just do homework. After she finished her homework, she could make a spaghetti sauce for dinner if she got started with defrosting hamburger right away. So she did that. She could call Margalo later, after Margalo's overnight guests had left and before her baby-sitting job started. Let Margalo stew for a while. It would serve her right for—they *could* have called last night, couldn't they? Just taken a short break from their fun to call. Mikey started on homework.

She was partway through the science reading—who *cared* how rocks were formed?—when the phone rang, and she had to race from her usual homework locale at the kitchen table to go out to the living room and answer it. She got there just before the machine picked up. "Hello?"

"Mikey?" The male voice sounded surprised. "It's me, Hon. I didn't think you'd be—I was calling to leave a message. In case you got back early and I wasn't . . ."

"Hi, Dad," she said when he didn't finish what he had started to say. But he seemed to have turned his head away from the phone and to be talking to someone else, telling someone else, "She's home already."

"Dad? Where are you?"

"At the office."

"What time did you go in?"

"I wasn't planning to come home until—I'll be home by one."

"No problem," Mikey said.

"She must have driven you home herself?"

"Nine thirty," Mikey told him.

"Well, so now you can make tennis practice," he said. "Do you want to?"

"Yeah. I would." It would feel good to be swinging her racquet and hitting the ball. A few overhead smashes—she imagined it—would feel pretty slime-ing good.

"I'll be home in a little while—if that's OK? Mikey, there's someone I'd like you to meet. Would you like to meet someone?"

Mikey knew what he was asking: Did she want to meet some woman he was dating? Who was probably the person in the background. Who was probably some woman at work and also probably—because her dad didn't lie to her—the reason why he hadn't told her how early he'd gone in that morning. She didn't want to hear or think any more about that.

"What do you say, Hon?" he asked.

She kept it short. Clear. "No."

"Some other time," he said.

*Uh-oh*, Mikey thought. "Mom's getting married Thursday."

There was a silence. Then, "You've met this man, do you like him all right?"

"He's rich. He's older. She said we don't have to worry about child support."

"Hunh," her father said. "How much older?"

"She's moving to Dallas."

"How rich?"

"Pretty."

"Hunh," he said again. Then out of the blue he asked, "Do I want to meet him?"

What was all of this meeting of people? "I'm cooking spaghetti sauce," Mikey told her father, and hung up.

Without thinking, Mikey punched 1 on speed dial. "Esther," she said. "Get me Margalo and don't give me any lip."

"It's Susannah," the girl's voice said.

"You heard me." Mikey didn't care who got Margalo, as long as it was quick.

Margalo said, "I can't talk, Mikey."

"My father wants me to meet someone."

"You're kidding."

"Not."

"Your parents are falling in love like there's no tomorrow," Margalo said.

"Can they still fall in love at their age?"

"They're still human," Margalo said. "At any age."

"My mom's getting married this week."

"Oh," Margalo said. She thought. "I might get home too late to call you."

"She bought me a dress. For the dance," Mikey said.

"Guilty conscience? Listen, Mikey, I really have to—"

"OK. See you," Mikey said, and hung up.

Sometimes she was sorry she'd talked Margalo into a career in baby-sitting. Sometimes it was inconvenient when Margalo was always off earning money.

Mikey went back to finish her homework, and then she got to work on the spaghetti sauce. She chopped and sautéed onions, adding garlic at the very end. She crumbled ground meat into the pan and browned it. She stirred in tomato paste and water, canned tomatoes, basil, oregano, a bay leaf, salt and pepper, and set the heat under the pot as low as it would go. While she washed up, the smell of the sauce started to fill

157

the kitchen, rich and tomatoey, a nourishing smell, the smell of Sunday evening—homework done, three hours of tennis adding to her normal appetite, her dad across the table and both of them talking, slurping spaghetti into their mouths.

She still had a couple of hours before practice, so Mikey went to unpack her suitcase.

Of course, the phone rang as soon as she got into her room. She was spending her whole life running for the phone. "Hello," she said, not exactly friendly.

"Mikey?"

"Who is this?" But she thought she recognized the voice. It might be him. Again. "Is this you again?" she demanded.

"I told you I'd call. So I can find out what you decided."

She bet she could figure out who this mysterious secret admirer was if she thought about it. If she felt like spending the time thinking about it, she could figure out this voice and get a face attached to it. "I didn't decide anything," she told him, deciding right then that maybe she'd gather some clues. "What do you want today?"

"You could tell me how your weekend went, at your mother's."

"How do you know I went to my mother's?"

He went on, as if she hadn't spoken, as if he'd planned what he was going to say and couldn't be distracted. "Because my parents are still married to each other, so I don't know what it's like to go visit one or the other of them. To be a guest in one parent's new house. What do you do when you're, like, a guest? I mean, not just their kid, in their house."

Mikey sat down. She'd never thought of it that way. "Go out for dinner with her and her dates. Go clothes shopping."

"*You* like shopping for clothes?"

"No. But she does, so it's what we do."

"What did you get?"

"This weekend? For me, a dress for the dance."

He hesitated. Asked, "You're going to the dance?"

"Of course not."

"Then why—"

"If you know me so grime-ing well, you already know why."

"She wants you to go to the dance?" he guessed.

"Bingo!" cried Mikey, loud and sarcastic.

"So your tennis matches must be pretty stressful for her."

"Is this Ralph?"

"Ralph?" he asked. "Ralph who?" he asked. "Ralph Nader?"

"Very funny," Mikey said.

He wasn't going to tell her who he was. And actually, that was OK with Mikey. She liked not knowing. It made him into a ghost, easy to talk to. "Don't feel sorry for my mom," she said. "She's getting married. This Thursday."

"Oh. I guess that's the real reason why you have a new dress."

"I'm not going to that wedding," she told him.

"You don't like the man she's marrying?"

"I'm not invited," she told him.

"You're kidding."

She didn't say anything.

"You're not kidding."

She didn't say anything.

"Don't you mind?" he asked.

"It's only a wedding. It's small, just a few friends, it isn't like—it doesn't have anything to do with me."

"You're really not kidding," he said.

The conversation was getting boring.

"I'd mind," he said. "I'd mind a lot."

She explained. "If I was there, it would just be her usual stuff, but it would be more of it because it's her perfect wedding to her ideal man."

"What do you mean, usual stuff?" he asked. He sounded interested, so she told him.

"The usual mother stuff. Stand up straight, pull in your stomach, look like you're having a good time, at least try. Don't talk about this, don't eat that way, why can't you try. I already got a lot of it this weekend, because she's packing and I couldn't do anything right."

"Not even books?"

"Not even books."

"What can you do wrong with books?"

"Get them out of order. Put them in the wrong way. Label the boxes wrong."

"Well," he said. "Well. Do you know what I think?"

"How could I know that?"

"She sounds to me like—all that criticism—she sounds like someone who doesn't want to feel bad about what she's doing. So she turns it into things wrong with you."

"Is this Margalo?" Mikey demanded.

"No," he said, and laughed. "So how are things going with Shawn?" he asked.

"Oh," she said. A memory of Shawn's face came to her, like looking at a photograph. She looked at the memory. "Well," she admitted, "he says we're just friends. Which I'm not, and I told him I wasn't, but—oh, trash it," she said.

"What is it about him, anyway?"

Mikey tried to explain. "What it is, is—Shawn—you look at him and you know—he's something special," she said. "You can't miss it. You see him and you just know. . . ."

After a little silence, "Maybe you have to be a girl," he said.

"I'm tired of this conversation," Mikey said. "I'm hanging up."

"I had an idea about your Chez ME cookies," he said quickly. "Listen to this," and now his voice got all enthusiastic. "I was thinking about how you might expand your business. Of course, you'd have to figure out packaging—"

This was actually interesting. "How would I find the time for a business?"

"School doesn't take that much, does it? Except sports, but—someone as smart as you, and Margalo, too—the thing is," he told her, "you'd have to upgrade some of your ingredients. Like the quality of the chocolate chips."

"What do you know about chocolate chips?"

"You can find all kinds of stuff on the Internet. Or, I was thinking, if you got your cookies into some regular commercial outlet—"

Mikey could see what he meant, but she didn't want to hear anything more from him until she had figured out what she thought for herself. "I've gotta go," she said.

"No, but listen," he said. His voice had gotten a little higher, as he hurried to tell her all of his ideas, and not so smooth. She almost recognized him now. "I've been thinking about it."

"So it seems."

And then, as if he was a car whose brakes had been jammed on by its driver, his words slowed down and his voice deepened again, and he said, "Not seems, *is*," with a smile in his voice as if that was some joke.

Mikey hung up.

She checked the spaghetti sauce, stirring it a little, thinking about stores where she might sell her cookies, and how she would get deliveries made. Then she went into her bathroom and dumped the laundry hamper out onto the floor, sorting her dirty clothes into lights and darks. What was wrong with her chocolate chips, anyway? Nothing, that was what. She didn't know about a couple of the new tops, so she had to find the little tag, hidden along a seam, to read the directions. She'd never had anything labeled Delicate before. She'd have to ask Margalo exactly what delicate meant, for doing laundry. Because she might just get rid of these delicate tops if they were going to be all that much trouble to clean.

She was jamming clothes into the washing machine in the utility room behind the kitchen, imagining how impressed Shawn would be if there was a newspaper article about Chez ME cookies and her business, when the phone rang.

Again.

"Hello," she said, irritated.

"Is Mikey there?"

This voice she knew. Her knees buckled a little with surprise. She dropped down onto the desk chair, holding the phone to her ear with both hands.

"Shawn? It's me."

She heard noises behind his voice, as if he was at a party.

"Where are you?" she asked him.

"I told you, the Mall."

"Who's with you?" she asked.

"Just some people. Listen, Mikey, I want to ask you. I mean, you're the one who'd know, I figure. Do you think Margalo would go to the dance with me?"

"Why?" *Ask Margalo to the dance?*

"If I asked her."

"Margalo?" *Why Margalo?*

"What do you think she'd say?"

He was distracted by a voice from behind him asking him something, which gave Mikey a little time. She worked it out like a math problem: Margalo did not have a crush on Shawn. In fact, sometimes Mikey suspected that Margalo didn't even like him. Also, Margalo had never said anything that indicated

163

that she might want to go to the dance at all. So if Shawn asked her, she'd say no.

"No," Mikey said.

"What?" he asked. "I couldn't hear you."

"No," Mikey said again. "Margalo wouldn't go to the dance with you."

"I don't believe you," Shawn said. "She's been working with me, you know, in rehearsals."

*What?* Margalo hadn't told her that.

She said, "You asked me what I think, and I told you."

"Well, I guess I have to take your word for it," he said. "Since you two are best friends. Is she going with someone else?" he asked, and then started to cough, a dry, choky cough, as if he was having trouble catching his breath.

"You OK?" she asked, and waited. When he'd stopped coughing and said, "Fine now," she asked him, "You don't already have a date? Because you could take me. As a friend," she said.

"Well, I don't know how good of a friend you are when you tell me not to ask Margalo but say *you'll* go with me."

"Is that a no?" Mikey demanded.

"Yes."

"Yes a no? Or plain yes?"

"Don't be any weirder than you can help," he advised her, and hung up.

So it was probably a no.

Well, *sewage*—but it wasn't as if she was surprised he

turned her down. It wasn't as if just because Margalo wouldn't go with him, he'd want to take Mikey. It wasn't as if she didn't know that. She knew it, she just didn't plan to lose out for lack of trying. Win or lose, lack of trying wasn't the way she liked to do things.

Before she had to think too hard about this last phone call and whether she should be proud (because Shawn had asked her advice) or angry (at Margalo, for getting him) or embarrassed (about being turned down), Mikey punched speed dial 1 and asked for Aurora. "When Margalo gets home, tell her she has to call me. It's really important," she told Margalo's mother.

"You always say things are really important," Aurora pointed out.

"I won't talk long," Mikey promised. "When's she coming home?"

"By nine. It's a school night," Aurora reminded her. "I'll tell her, Mikey."

"Good," Mikey said.

"We aim to please." Aurora sounded like she wanted to laugh. "Later, Mikey," and she hung up. That was where Margalo probably got all of her jokes from, her mother, who couldn't even get off the phone like a normal mother.

Mikey could imagine how relieved Margalo would be to hear that Mikey had saved her from going to the dance. She thought Margalo might have some interesting things to say about why Shawn would want to ask her. She was glad she was going to play three hours of tennis, drills and then some games, so she could concentrate on something besides Shawn Macavity. Sometimes it was no fun at all to think about him. And it would definitely be no fun waiting around at home for Margalo to call so Mikey could get Margalo's opinion about the call from Shawn.

Margalo's opinion was: "Why would you do something like that? What is the *matter* with you, Mikey?"

"Do you *want* to go to this scummy dance? What about *me*?"

"Oh, never mind," Margalo said, and hung up.

Mikey slammed the phone down and her father looked away from the television to ask her, "What dance?"

# WEEK THREE

## GIRL LOSES BOY

# 12
# ALL GIRLS IN LOVE ARE BAD

Margalo had thought about it, and thought about it. And thought some more about it.

Finally she decided not to yell at Mikey, because what good would that do? When she got off the school bus that Monday morning, the last Monday before the dance, she had a plan, which did *not* include talking to Mikey about the incredibly loamy thing Mikey had done.

So Margalo got off the bus and met up with Mikey as usual. It was snowing lightly, not enough to close down schools, but there was always hope that it would start coming down more heavily and they would have one of those chaotic days with shortened classes. The morning news had predicted a tapering off by midmorning, but there *was* a faint chance.

Mikey was making a big deal of it. "Do you think school will close early? What about tomorrow?"

169

"In your dreams," Margalo said. She hunched her shoulders against the cold and headed for the door.

"Not that I *want* to miss school," Mikey told her. "Because how would I see Shawn?"

Margalo shrugged.

"What's wrong with you? You aren't mad at me, are you? I'm the one who should be mad at you," Mikey pointed out.

They stepped inside, where immediately it was too hot.

"I'm not really mad," Margalo said. "Only sort of."

"You shouldn't be angry at all," Mikey told her. "Unless—" and she stopped, wheeling around to stare right into Margalo's face, grabbing Margalo's coat and forcing Margalo to a halt. "He told me you've been rehearsing with just him. You didn't tell me that. You aren't in lurve with him too, are you?"

"With Shawn?" Margalo could have laughed. Her life would look a lot brighter, and there would be things she could do, if it was Shawn she had her hopeless crush on. But she didn't laugh; instead, she considered possible responses, ways to get even with Mikey, by pretending Shawn was chasing her, or telling Mikey her real opinion of Shawn. But in the end all Margalo said was the simple truth. "No."

They started moving along again. "So you *can't* care about going to the dance with him," Mikey pointed out.

"I *don't* care about going with *him*," Margalo agreed. "But I'd have liked to go."

"What are you talking about?" Mikey demanded. "You

don't mean that," she decided, explaining to Margalo, "You're just saying that to try to make me feel bad. Well, I don't."

Margalo had more important things to do than telling Mikey off. She had her own plans. Hurriedly she took off her coat.

"She got me a dress for the dance," Mikey said. "It was our only break from packing. You're wearing your dog's throw-up sweater."

"Yes." Margalo hung her coat in the locker.

"To build confidence?"

"Because it looks good on me," Margalo said. She picked out the books and papers she'd need for her morning classes.

"I was going to say that next."

"I bet you were."

"So what?" Mikey demanded.

They didn't say anything more on that subject, and eventually Margalo, now ready to leave, asked, "What were you packing?"

"Her apartment. So she can move. After she gets married. To Dallas." Mikey was thumping books into her locker, thumping books down onto the floor, as she spoke. "This week."

"This week?" Surprise kept Margalo where she was.

"Thursday."

Margalo considered this. "Married or moving Thursday?"

"Married. She's moving over the weekend. Next weekend,

171

when the dance is. That's why I had to go there this one."

"So the dress is for the wedding," Margalo deduced.

Mikey shook her head. "Why would I want to go to the wedding where my mother marries someone besides my father? Someone old enough to be a grandfather."

Margalo guessed, "She didn't ask you, did she?" What was *wrong* with Mikey's mother?

"So what?"

"That slime-ing stinks," Margalo said. Not that she was surprised. "That stinks big time. Aurora should have custody of you, that's what I think."

"You can keep that thought to yourself," Mikey said. "I never saw a mother I wanted, including my own. That's not funny," she told Margalo.

"I know," Margalo said, but couldn't stop grinning. "It isn't a bit funny. But it's really funny anyway. Listen, I've gotta go talk to Hadrian—about the play. He's going to be stage manager and I have to tell him."

"Hadrian? The stage manager? I didn't know there was a stage manager job open."

"It's not anymore." Margalo knew what Mikey was thinking, so she reminded her, "You have basketball practice Monday, Tuesday, Wednesday, and Thursday."

"I can skip that."

"Sometimes you have games."

"Almost never. I could easily be stage manager."

"We can argue about it later," Margalo said, holding her

books close to her chest, sprinting away down the hall to talk to Hadrian before she got to work on the real business of her morning.

The real business was Shawn. If he still wanted to ask her to the dance. If he was going to, if Mikey hadn't entirely ruined her chances. She spoke briefly to Hadrian and then went to find Shawn outside his homeroom, at the center of a mass of both girls and boys. Margalo made her way through to him, saying, "Excuse me, excuse me," and holding up the script of the play. "I need to talk with you," she said to Shawn.

"Hey, Margalo, whazzup?" he asked, and smiled lazily, looking around him for confirmation of his unspoken statement: *Here comes another one.*

"It's about the play." She waved the script in front of his eyes. "It'll only take—"

"Oh." Did he look disappointed? Or was he acting? "OK."

She made her way back through the group, which already didn't have any time to waste on her, and he followed. "Don't go far," they said to Shawn. "Don't take long."

"So, what is it?" Shawn asked her. "What's so important it can't wait for rehearsal?"

Margalo's plan was to have a normal conversation. Just in case, just to give him a chance to ask her. She wasn't going to bring up the subject of the dance; but if there was only the two of them, he *could* ask her, if he wanted to. In normal conversation mode she told him, "I probably won't be working with you today. To hear your lines. Or anymore, maybe."

Now he definitely was disappointed. "Why? What'd I do?"

"Ms. Larch will be going over your lines with you. To hear how you're doing," she said.

For about half a minute he didn't say anything, just stared in the direction of her face. There was no seeing taking place, however.

Margalo waited.

"OK," he said finally. "Thanks for the warning, Margalo."

She shrugged.

He waited, in case there was something else she wanted to say to him, and she waited, in case there was something he wanted to ask her, until he finally wondered, "You talk to Mikey since yesterday?"

"Yes," she said. Steven said guys hate to ask someone out and get turned down, and Howie and David wouldn't admit it, but they acted like they felt the same. Margalo tried to think of what she might say to let Shawn know that Mikey got it wrong, that she would definitely accept his invitation to the dance.

"I figured, you two talk all the time," Shawn said.

"You were right," she said. She was opening her mouth to add a hint (*Even if Mikey wasn't right, you were*), when he looked straight into her eyes, still waiting for her to say something. To say what? What could he be expecting her to say? Margalo had no idea. But he wasn't looking at her like someone who wanted to invite her to any dance.

She stared back into his blue eyes—guessing and ruling

out guesses. It felt like a long time before he said, "So, I guess you and Mikey are pretty good friends. Like, always sticking together. That must get hard, I mean for you, I mean sometimes."

Then Margalo had her idea: So *that* was what he was playing at. But why would he want to break up a friendship between two girls he couldn't care less about? She couldn't answer that, but she *could* outplay Shawn Macavity, at any game. She could outplay him with one hand tied behind her back, and blindfolded, and her left cerebral hemisphere out of commission.

"Not really," she told him. Then she said, "I hope you learned at least the first three scenes over the weekend, like you told me you would. I told Ms. Larch you'd said you'd know it by today," she said. And smiled at him in a friendly fashion, like someone who was on his side and wished him well, but she kept the smile on her face long after its expiration date so he would know she actually wished him the opposite and was smiling at the thought of how much trouble he was going to be in with Ms. Larch. And left him standing there.

All right. That finished Shawn. She was still angry at Mikey, but she knew part of the reason was that even if she told Mikey her guess—that Shawn wanted to see if he could get them quarreling over him—Mikey wouldn't admit what a slime-ing, slime-ball, slime-brained person she was in lurve with.

Margalo wasn't about to say much of anything to Mikey about this. People weren't interested in contradictory opinions of people they were in lurve with. Besides, since Margalo in fact had a lot of sympathy for Mikey's situation, she didn't mind keeping quiet on the subject.

Meanwhile, Mikey was relieved when Margalo headed off to talk to Hadrian. She hadn't seen Shawn since Friday, and she was ready to have him in her sights. She slung her book bag over her shoulder and went on along the hallway to Mrs. Brannigan's homeroom.

Mikey went down the hall, concealed in the midst of a crowd. When she glimpsed Shawn standing near the homeroom doorway, she went on for a few paces and then turned to join the crowd of people moving in the opposite direction, to see Shawn from the other side, see him again. But Shawn had moved—had he entered the homeroom?—and for a few seconds she lost him. Then she saw him, across the hallway, and it was Margalo he was talking to. Mikey knew that dog's throw-up sweater. She also knew what Margalo was doing: Telling Shawn yes, she would go to the dance with him. Which wasn't *fair.*

But they said, All's fair in love and war.

They might say that, but they still hold trials for war criminals, so *they* didn't think it was true either, and it really *wasn't* fair for Margalo to do this without even telling Mikey.

The first bell rang then and she had to get to homeroom,

or she would have gone right up to say something to Margalo, right then, right there. But she had to wait until they were leaving homeroom. "I saw you talking to him," she said to Margalo as they parted at the door. "I know what you did."

"No you don't," Margalo said.

"Are you going to the dance with him?"

"I'm not going to the dance with anyone, thanks to you."

"I *saw* you. You were talking to him."

"I was warning him that he'll be rehearsing with Ms. Larch, not me. He hasn't been learning his lines, and I can't make him." Margalo said that as if Mikey was an irritating idiot not to know that already.

"Oh," Mikey said. Then, "I bet *I* could. I bet if I was the stage manager I could manage Shawn. I should have been stage manager," she told Margalo.

"You know you'd be a terrible stage manager for a play that has Shawn Macavity in it," Margalo told her, not even thinking for half a second about the possibility.

Maybe Mikey could persuade Hadrian to give up the position. In fifth grade Margalo'd said he had a crush on Mikey, and last year, too, so maybe if she asked him, he would. But even if Hadrian did give it up, Margalo would probably think of some reason for Mikey not to get to do it. In fact, there was no maybe about it, because wasn't that what Margalo just said?

Sludge on Margalo, anyway. She was being a real grump.

But Mikey couldn't get too worked up about Margalo, because she couldn't deny that she *had* ruined Margalo's chances of being asked to the dance by Shawn Macavity. She hadn't meant to ruin anything, but she had. So if Margalo wanted to get even, Mikey couldn't blame her.

"I don't blame you," Mikey said as they shifted books in the break between periods two and three.

"Well, that's a big relief," Margalo said, sarcastic.

Mikey had had about enough of Margalo's bad mood. "What's *wrong* with you?"

"Nothing," Margalo said. "Nothing's wrong."

"I don't believe you."

"Go ahead, don't. It's a free country."

Then Margalo turned to catch up with Casey Wolsowski, to go to their A-level English class together, and be smart at English together. Tall, skinny Margalo and short, squat Casey made a funny-looking pair. They looked like an illustration from a grade-school math book: *This is a square and this is a line.* Margalo didn't even wave a hand at Mikey or say *See you.* She just walked away.

At last, Mikey got it: Margalo was angry. She guessed maybe Margalo did want to go to the dance. But how was Mikey supposed to know that? Margalo had never said.

OK, but now that she did know, what could she do about it?

That question occupied her for the rest of the morning, and the answer she came up with pleased her: She would talk to Shawn. After all, he'd said they were friends. He meant just friends, only friends, she knew, but that was still friends, wasn't it? Friends could ask favors of each other and talk about their problems with other friends.

At lunch Mikey moved quickly, not looking around so as not to get joined up with Margalo. She moved along the length of the cafeteria line until she saw Shawn between a couple of boys, but before she could get close enough to talk to him, somebody in line called her name—Ralph—and he reached out to grab her by the arm. "Did you decide?"

"Decide what?" she asked back, and then she remembered. "About tennis," she told him.

"Mind like a steel trap," he said to Ira, in line behind him.

Mikey hadn't even thought about it, but now she decided. "Sure," she said. "I'll do it."

"Good," he said. "We'll be good. You know? We'll make, like, the winning team."

"If you work on your net game, we will."

"And humble, too," Ralph said to Ira.

"Especially the high backhands," Mikey told him.

She got going again, heading for Shawn, but Cassie got there ahead of her. Cassie stood blocking Shawn's way, her tray held out in front of her. They stood tray to tray.

"Tooth!" Cassie cried as if she was surprised he was there, even though with her full tray and his empty one she must have walked into him on purpose. "Put me out of my misery," she requested.

Shawn smiled; he was cool. He glanced around at his audience before he said, "Gladly. Are you thinking of a bullet in the brain?"

"Ha," Cassie said. "Ha, ha. Very witty, Tooth. That's not what I was talking about, of course, but you get an A for effort."

"So what were you talking about?" he asked.

"I meant"—she leaned forward, her spiky hair practically brushing his cheek—"you should tell us who the lucky girl is."

Shawn leaned back and asked, "Lucky girl?" He glanced around with raised eyebrows, wordlessly asking his audience, were they as puzzled as he was?

"Who you're taking to the dance," Cassie said. "The world wonders."

"Oh," Shawn said. "That." He smiled, teasing, mysterious—Mona Lisa except in a Hawaiian shirt, and a guy. "Well," he said. "She could be you if I didn't happen to know for a fact that you already have a date. With Jace," he reminded her. "Isn't that right, Jace?" he called into the cafeteria.

Mikey didn't know *what* to think. Why was Shawn talking as if he wanted to ask Cassie to the dance?

He'd surprised Cassie into having nothing to say. She stared into his face and didn't say one word. Then she walked slowly away, and he moved on down the line, and the audience got back to their own affairs.

Mikey decided maybe she'd wait to talk to Shawn about Margalo until after she got Margalo's opinion about what had just happened. But Margalo wasn't at their table. In fact, she hadn't seen Margalo since midmorning. Frannie was seated at the table, reading, and Casey was there too. Casey just couldn't believe what she'd heard, and wanted Mikey's opinion, because Shawn should be really mad at Cassie for the mean and mocking and hostile way she always talked to him, didn't Mikey agree?

Margalo never showed up for lunch, but only Mikey seemed to notice her absence. Casey talked away at Mikey about Shawn until she interrupted herself to say, "Look!" and Mikey saw that Cassie was hurrying to catch up to Shawn, who was on his way out of the cafeteria. "Do you think he *will* ask her?" Casey asked.

"Who?" Frannie wondered. She'd finished catching up on her reading for seminar. "Do I think who'll ask who?" Frannie was going with a group of kids. They were having a pizza dinner first at Jason's house, then all going on to the dance together.

"Look," Casey said again. "There," she pointed.

They watched Shawn listen to whatever Cassie was saying, saw him smile widely at her. He shook his head and said one short word that you didn't have to be a skilled lip-reader to know was *No.* Then she said something more, and he shrugged, opening his hands carelessly out into the air, *I didn't do anything.* Then Cassie said something furious furiously—if her words matched her face, they were some of Mr. Saunders's least favorite vocabulary choices. Shawn's face

181

mocked shock and he wagged a forefinger at her, *Tsk-tsk.*
Cassie flung herself out of the room.

Frannie looked at Casey and then at Mikey, and then she looked around the table they were sitting at. "What happened to Margalo?" she asked. "Where is she?"

# 13
# ALTHOUGH SOME
# ARE WORSE THAN OTHERS

Margalo was in the upstairs girls' bathroom.

Sometimes she just wanted to be alone, because sometimes the sadness of the thing overwhelmed her, this hopeless lurve of hers. In the second-floor bathroom, in the end stall, with the door latched shut and its bolt slid into place, she pulled down the toilet lid and sat. She held her books in a pile on her lap. She had her brown bag lunch on top of the books. She sat there, locked in, being alone.

She wasn't really crying. She was just oozing a little.

She'd be fine in time for seminar—she knew that—but she wasn't fine yet.

She reached into her lunch bag and took out the peanut butter and jelly sandwich she'd packed that morning. She must have forgotten to put a thin layer of peanut butter on the jelly side of the bread, because it was soaked purple, and limp. It looked as dismal as she felt.

Margalo oozed and chewed, hunched over the pile of books, oozed and chewed and swallowed. What kind of life was it anyway, when the only place you could be alone was the bathroom?

Then—she heard it with alarm—the heavy bathroom door opened. Margalo swallowed quickly and pulled up her feet, jamming her books uncomfortably into her chest. She wrapped her arms around her ankles and sat there, waiting for whoever it was to go away.

If anyone tried the stall door, they wouldn't be able to open it. They'd probably think it was stuck, or broken.

The intruder was a bunch of girls, who all came in together. Margalo heard feet moving around and in her thin line of visibility glimpsed two pairs of Hush Puppies and their skirts, then a pair of Nikes at the end of a pair of jeans; she heard the clumpy sound of boots. The different dress styles didn't surprise her. These days, in eighth grade, cliques didn't stick so exclusively together. If your boyfriend, for example, was friends with somebody whose girlfriend was in a different clique, you and that girl could get to be friends too. These intruders entered all talking at once, mentioning no names, offering Margalo no clues.

Then she heard a sound she half recognized, and when she smelled tobacco she could name it: A lighter being flicked on.

"I didn't know you smoked," a voice said.

"I didn't used to," someone answered. Someone Margalo

knew—but who? "I don't smoke much," this someone said.

Margalo's sadness was being swept aside by curiosity. She sat very still and tried to identify the voice.

"But when you've got a high school boyfriend"—Ronnie, then; yes, Ronnie. Well, well—"it's useful to have a cigarette sometimes. If you know what I mean," Ronnie said.

A couple of low, sophisticated murmurs, until somebody else asked, "Smoking's so bad for you, and everybody around you, how can it be useful?"

"A cigarette buys time, when he's putting pressure on you to—oh, I don't even want to talk about it. I'm giving cigarettes up, as soon as—this is my last cigarette. I'm just . . . see, guys, Sophie's going to tell Doug, today if she sees him, tomorrow for sure because they have yearbook—Sophie's going to tell him I want to break up with him."

"What about the dance?" was the urgent question. "He was taking you to the dance."

There was an exhaling sound. Margalo had a mouthful of mushed-up peanut butter and jelly, so she swallowed now—noiselessly, she hoped.

"I told him already I wasn't going to the dance with him," Ronnie said.

"When?"

"Why?"

"But it's Saturday, how will you—"

"Do you have another date?"

As Margalo pictured it, Ronnie was smiling and shaking her head, Miss Queen of Mysterious. Finally Ronnie spoke again. "If I tell you, you have to promise—"

"I promise. We do."

"—not to tell anyone. Until *we* tell—until then, do you promise?"

"We do."

"I do."

"Cross my heart."

After a long pause Ronnie spoke. "It's Shawn. I'm going to the dance with Shawn."

There was a moment's stunned silence. Everybody in the bathroom—*everybody*, not just the invisible girls probably leaning against the sinks and looking into the mirrors—was stunned. Shocked. Chagrined. And in one case, enlightened.

"*Ronnie*," they protested.

"Really?" they asked.

"Shawn Macavity?"

"You and Shawn?"

"Since when?"

Margalo, coiled on the toilet seat, listened alertly. She heard water being run, just a little burst of water. She pictured Ronnie dousing her cigarette.

"Wow," three voices said, not quite in unison.

"Are you two—"

"Maybe," Ronnie said. "Probably."

"When did that happen?"

"He asked me first a couple of weeks ago. At that party of Heather's—before she—What happened was, we were dancing and he said he wished I could go to the dance with him, but he didn't want to break up a couple. I asked him, what made him so sure that was what he'd be doing? And he was so . . . glad. He was really glad to hear that."

"Wow."

"That's so romantic."

"The funny thing is, I'd only started flirting with Shawn at Rhonda's—the night before, remember?—because I wanted to make Doug jealous because he kept dissing me for being in eighth grade. Like he was such a superior life-form. So it's really his own fault."

"You've known for over a week you were breaking up with Doug?"

"No, of course not. No, really. At first I tried not to break up with Doug. I *tried* to make things work out. But you can't feel what you don't feel, can you? And then Shawn asked me again. It was at my party, Saturday—when all I could dance with was Doug, you know? Shawn said he'd been waiting all week, hoping I could go with him. So I said yes. Because . . . I really, really like him. I mean, *really*. He's so different from Doug. . . ." Her voice drifted dreamily off.

"You must be so happy."

"But first I have to dump Doug, don't I?"

"That's so *mean*," the words buried in giggles.

"Let's go," Ronnie said, and Margalo heard her explain as the door opened, "I told Shawn I'd be in the library after lunch."

Not all of them left, however, so Margalo stayed still, trapped where she was, and tightened her arms around her shins and listened.

"So, what kind of pressure do you think it was?"

"How far do you think she let him go?"

"I can't tell—can you?"

"She gets whoever she wants, so she's pretty sexy I guess. But do you think she's—"

"Nobody talks about her, none of the boys, and they would, don't you think?"

"Every boy worth wanting wants her."

"She's not all that pretty. Do you think she is?"

"She's got that great body."

"But Shawn, too? It's not fair. It's just not a bit fair. She doesn't need to have everyone."

"She just gets everyone. Anyone she wants."

"You heard her say she flirted on purpose. That's not fair either."

"She should have told us. Don't you think? We're her closest—and Casey, too. Especially Casey. She's supposed to be Casey's friend, and Casey writes him these poems."

"Only short poems. Only fourteen lines."

"And she gives them to him too."

"But he makes fun of them. You've heard him doing it."

"Ronnie should have told. It's really not fair. It's just not—and this school sucks, too. I am so sick of—"

"Me, too." A brief silence. "We could start a fire. You want to? Get out of a couple of classes?"

Margalo listened, perched and poised, and grinning away. This was better than a TV show. This was as good as a good book.

The door opened again, and a voice complained, "We're waiting. What're you doing in here?"

"We're debating starting a fire."

"Cool," they said, and "Why?" and "It'll get us out of science," and "I don't think we should," and "Why not?"

Then, "What if we get caught?" someone wondered, and "They'll blame a smoker," someone explained.

"Let's not," someone said, and "I don't want to anyway," and "We were joking anyway." They left the bathroom together, all of them.

Margalo took her time, lowering her feet, standing up, opening the door, leaving the room. She took her time at her locker, changing her books, and took her time meandering towards the seminar classroom, and was crossing by the library door just as Ronnie came out.

"Hey, Ronnie," she said. "How's Doug? You looking forward to showing him off at the dance?"

"Oh," Ronnie said. "Doug's Doug, you know." Then the bell rang and Ronnie said, "I have to—but how's the play?" she asked.

"Fine," Margalo said. "Everything's totally fine," she said, and meant it. This lunch had entirely cheered her up. Luckily for her, there was more to life than lurve.

Mikey didn't believe it. When Margalo told her about it on the telephone that night, "I don't know why you'd make up a story like that," she said. "Why didn't they see you?"

Margalo admitted she'd been in one of the stalls.

"They'd see your feet," Mikey pointed out.

"I pulled them up."

"And your books."

"They were on my lap."

"What were you *doing*?"

"Eating lunch."

"I can't believe you'd spend all lunch period sitting in a bathroom."

Finally Margalo said, "I just . . . I needed to be alone—what's wrong with that? I just . . . I wanted to cry a little, if it's any of your business. All right?"

"But why would you want to sit on a toilet and cry? What's *wrong* with you?"

"Nothing! There is nothing wrong with me. It's normal, perfectly normal to—haven't you ever heard of PMS?"

"You don't get that," Mikey reminded her.

"Or hormones?"

"You're having hormones? No wonder you're making up stories about Shawn and Ronnie. No wonder you won't admit

I'd be a good stage manager." And then Mikey had to listen to the many reasons she'd make a bad stage manager, until she could interrupt to tell Margalo that she'd heard at basketball that Louis Caselli was going to ask a seventh grader to the dance. Margalo hoped they'd all say no too, and Mikey hoped right along with her, and then Susannah called time on the call.

When Ronnie wore the team jacket to school the next day, Tuesday, Mikey gloated. "I told you so," she said. "Didn't I tell you?" At lunch she remembered to tell Margalo about what had happened between Cassie and Shawn in the cafeteria, "while you were having hormones yesterday. So that's more proof that Shawn doesn't have a date for the dance," she concluded. "So much for your made-up story."

But Margalo sounded pleased. "I thought so."

"That's not what you said," Mikey reminded her. "You said he was going with Ronnie."

"No, I mean I thought Cassie liked him. And that probably explains the way she and Jace were having such a big, serious conversation this morning."

Mikey tried again, patiently. "If Shawn already had a date, why would he be thinking about asking all of you other people?"

At that moment they saw Cassie and Jace enter the cafeteria together, pick up trays together, and stand in line together, Cassie behind Jace. Cassie did not look particularly cheerful, although Jace did.

"How would I know?" Margalo answered. "Unless he

wants to see how many girls would go with him. Like, some kind of test for how popular he is."

"That would be really stupid," Mikey pointed out.

Margalo didn't argue.

"Besides, he never asked me," Mikey said. "You know, he *could* be going alone. Or be in with a group, all going together."

"Or maybe *he'll* be Louis Caselli's date, but we won't find that out until Monday morning. Will we. We won't know anything until way after it happens. Thanks to you."

Mikey pointed out the obvious. "If he's just playing some game, he wasn't going to ask you anyway."

"That's not the point," Margalo said.

"So actually, I did you a favor. You should be grateful to me."

"Slag and sullage," Margalo said. "You weren't trying to do me any favors."

"Mudpies, Margalo. I was trying to do what I thought you wanted."

That, Margalo couldn't argue with, so she didn't.

"Maybe he'll ask me at the last minute," Mikey said, then, "When is too late? Saturday morning, do you think? Saturday afternoon?"

"*Now* is too late," Margalo advised her.

At which point, Cassie crashed her metal tray down on their table, causing some Beefaroni to slide off the plate and onto the tray. She jerked back a chair to plunk down on and picked up the spilled food with her fingers. She told Mikey and Margalo, "He forgives me. This is so depressing."

In Mikey's opinion, what was depressing was all the black Cassie was always wearing.

"What are you going to do?" Margalo asked.

"I told him I'd still go to the dance with him. But really—Jace is such a wimpoid—I didn't *ask* him to forgive me, you can be sure of that."

Mikey was relieved to hear it.

"But if someone wants to forgive you, you can't stop them, can you?" Cassie asked. "You can't make someone *not* forgive you any more than you can *make* them be in love with you."

"Or *not* be in love with you," Margalo agreed.

And what suddenly made Margalo the love expert?

Cassie said, "Besides, it's a known fact that kids our age can't really be in love."

"Lurve," Mikey claimed. "We can be in lurve."

Margalo said, "Juliet was thirteen."

Mikey turned on Margalo. "Don't bother telling me any more of your made-up stories." *About Shawn*, she didn't say. That went without saying. The trouble was, she knew that Margalo didn't make things up, not to her; Mikey and Margalo had always not told lies to each other, and Mikey knew that. But now, "Don't even try," she warned.

"You make up stories?" Cassie asked Margalo, immediately curious. "Do you write? Are you any good?"

Mikey watched Margalo decide how she would answer that question.

# 14
# WILL YOU—WON'T YOU— WILL YOU—WON'T YOU—WILL YOU JOIN THE DANCE?

It snowed Tuesday night and into Wednesday morning, a fine, steady snow that the wind sent drifting across plowed roads. They didn't get a snow day out of it, but they did get a delayed opening. Late opening meant confusion and chaos all day long. All the classes were shortened to half the usual time, so nobody was quite sure who was supposed to be where, or when, and the bells—which were electronically programmed for a normal day—had to be manually rung. Everybody already knew that human beings are not as efficient as electricity, and the bells offered more proof of that. People came to school ready for chaos on Wednesday morning, two hours later than usual, planning to enjoy themselves.

Cassie stopped by while Mikey and Margalo were stuffing their jackets into their lockers, to say, "This is gonna be fun," as if she meant it. Then she added, in case they got the wrong impression, "As much fun as school can ever be. All these little rooms, little boxes—did you ever think of how much classrooms resemble boxes? With the lids on?"

"No," Mikey said. "I never did. I don't think I will, either."

For the cold day Margalo had dressed in a long green corduroy skirt, with a flowery blouse on top, and she knew she looked old-fashioned, and she also thought that old-fashioned looked older, too, as in more mature. Mikey that day wore a V-necked tennis sweater, white with blue and red stripes at the bottom, over a dark blue turtleneck. Margalo commented without thinking, "Nice outfit."

"The fashion police approve," Mikey said, sarcastic.

"I mean you look organized," Margalo said.

"It's too preppy for me," Cassie remarked.

Mikey denied that. "Am not."

Cassie ignored her. "Must be the CK jeans."

"Tell you what," Mikey said, spreading her feet and putting her hands on her hips. "Let me tell you," she said, winding up for an R&R.

Margalo stepped back to enjoy this. She always liked to watch Cassie dangle the bait and Mikey rise to it and then, usually, swallow it whole—after which she often jerked Cassie into the water, the fish that got the fisherman.

Mikey folded her arms across her chest and started. "The urban look, you know? Urban black. Arty. The *I'm wearing black because I'm so sad and wise and generally superior to the rest of you clodpoles.* Black boots, black tights, black jeans, black tops—and why women make up their eyes to look like

Egyptian paintings, putting that thick black stuff—" She turned to Margalo.

"Kohl," Margalo supplied.

"Trying to look like something they're not, like they're exotic or on the stage or like they've been around . . ."

This was a new R&R topic, and Mikey hadn't refined her thoughts on the subject so she was stumbling around a little, looking for the flow.

"What you arty types wear is just another uniform," Mikey said. She was about to get going on that subject, when they noticed a curious kind of quiet coming down the hall at them. Like dominoes falling over, each domino knocking the next one over, the students crowding the hallway with noise fell silent, one after another, the silence moving from the big entrance doors next to the *A* lockers down through the alphabet toward the *E*s.

"Whazzis?" Cassie asked them. But as soon as they turned and looked, they could see what it was. Or, who.

A young man—actually, a boy, as they looked at him more closely—marched down the hallway. He wore a down vest, jeans, work boots, and a determined expression. He was a perfectly ordinary boy, sort of cute, with a short nose and broad cheekbones, thick, short hair—and older.

"What do you bet Doug?" Margalo murmured to Mikey.

"Oh, I hope so," Cassie said softly.

"Where's Ronnie?" Mikey asked.

Ronnie stood in front of her locker among a group of

friends, a couple of whom wore shoes that Margalo recognized. Ronnie's shiny, dark hair rested on the blue shoulders of the team jacket. She saw the young man before he saw her, and her eyes widened in alarm.

He strode on down the hallway—people stepping aside to let him go through—scanning faces to find the one he was looking for. He was bigger than the seventh- and eighth-grade boys—bigger arms, bigger legs, taller, wider chest, thicker neck, longer feet—bigger and stronger, and he walked like someone who knows where he's going, even though they could all see he didn't know exactly where he was going.

Then he saw her. "Hey, Babe," he called. This was a confident greeting, but his voice didn't sound confident. "Look who's here," he said, spreading out his arms.

Ronnie pretended not to hear him. She pretended to be in some deep and fascinating conversation with Annie Piers—the only friend who hadn't slipped back into the crowd of students in the hallway when they heard the approaching silence and saw Doug. Annie stood in front of Ronnie with her books clutched up against her chest, nodding her head at whatever Ronnie was saying, nodding even when Ronnie wasn't saying anything.

Nice people with good manners went on to their homerooms. There weren't very many of those, so the hallway stayed crowded with normal, not-so-nice people who wanted everybody to think they had good manners, trying to look like they were talking to one another. Mikey sidled up as close as she could get to Ronnie's locker, and Margalo went with her. They didn't want to miss anything. Cassie stuck with them.

"Babe," Doug said in a louder and deeper voice than middle-school boys possessed. "I wanna say, no hard feelings."

Then he seemed to notice there were other people around. It was Annie he focused on. "Do you mind?" he asked her. "This is a private conversation."

Annie glanced at Ronnie and clutched her books tighter. "I have to . . . it's . . . I'll see you," she mumbled, backing off, then turning around to disappear into the crowd.

This left Ronnie alone, her chin raised, her dark hair gleaming. She looked like Bambi's mother, noble and help-less. She looked like Joan of Arc, defiant and helpless. She looked right at Doug and then over his shoulder, looking down the hall, moving farther along the alphabet.

Margalo turned to see where Shawn Macavity leaned against his locker door, watching Ronnie. This was better than any soap opera she might have watched if it had in fact been a snow day. Margalo turned back to Mikey's eager face, and both of them raised their eyebrows—eyebrows up, eyebrows down—in anticipation.

Doug came close to Ronnie and leaned one muscular arm beside her head, resting the palm of the hand against a closed locker. "I like to say my goodbye's in person," he said. "Also, you have my jacket."

"I didn't want it anyway." Ronnie pulled one arm free of the jacket and let it fall off of one shoulder, while she got her other arm out of it. The jacket dropped onto the floor and lay there like a dark blue puddle with the name *Doug* floating on it.

Doug bent down and picked it up. "That's more like it," he said, as if announcing a victory. "Thanks a lot, Ronnie," he said to her back. "You were a whole lot of fun." Then he looked around at his audience, hesitating before he added the finishing touch to his thought. "*Not.*"

By this time nobody was pretending to be doing anything else but watching, and Doug watched back now, scanning the faces. "Which one of them will you go to this dorkmobile dance with now, Babe? She's available, guys," he said, and strode out, strode back down the hall and through the doors, which clanged shut behind him.

Ronnie leaned her forehead against the closed locker next to her open one. Her shoulders moved and everybody could see how distressed she was. Shawn Macavity got to her first. He put his arm around her and pulled her to him. She followed his lead, as if they were dancing a slow dance, rotating until she could bury her face in his shoulder. He bent his head over her, protectively, like Thomas Mendip saving Jennet Jourdemayne in the last scene of *The Lady's Not for Burning*.

Everybody watching was totally amazed and totally surprised. Everyone, that is, except for Ronnie's six best friends, and Margalo, and Mikey.

Everybody knew that when he spoke, what Shawn said

was, "You're going to the dance with me." They knew it even if they couldn't hear it.

Ronnie raised her face then, eyes shining through tears that spilled down her cheeks.

"When I cry, my nose runs," Cassie muttered. "And I think I drool, too."

Ronnie nodded her head and smiled, and everybody thought—from the looks on the faces of the two—that they were watching the first moment of the year's big romance. Everybody, that is, except Ronnie's six best friends, and Margalo, and Mikey.

Margalo restrained herself from asking Mikey, "What did I tell you?" She figured, this couldn't be one of Mikey's happiest moments. She thought, Mikey must be feeling like sort of a jerk. Then she thought, *No sort-of about it.*

But when she looked at Mikey's face, there was that same old goopy expression on it. Mikey was looking at Shawn Macavity as if he was some big hero who had acted with incredible bravery and saved the day, saved the girl, saved the world.

Cassie had slouched off, thoroughly disgusted, but Casey Wolsowski was coming up to say to Mikey, sisters in suffering, "I guess we don't have any chance at all now, do we?"

"What are you talking about?" Mikey demanded, but didn't give Casey any time to answer before she said to Margalo, "You'd think he'd be smart enough not to fall for a pretty face. Wouldn't you?"

"No," Margalo told her.

Mikey knew what Margalo wasn't saying. She also couldn't help but notice how this new development matched up to Margalo's previous information. But that didn't make any difference to her. She agreed with Margalo that it ought to make a difference—although Margalo didn't say that, either—but she didn't feel any change in how she felt.

Margalo must have figured that out too, because she only talked about Doug, and what high school boys might be like, if he was any example, then about the seminar reading and the science unit test, telling Mikey (again!—as if she hadn't heard this 325 times already) about how interesting Mr. Schramm's tests were, and how fair and how carefully graded. But at least Margalo could talk about something besides Ronnie and Shawn, which was all everybody else was interested in that morning, saying how Ronnie and Shawn had been just friends until—*kaboom!*—they looked at each other and just *knew*.

At the abbreviated, late-opening lunch Casey sat with Mikey and Margalo, not at her usual lunch table among her usual lunch companions, which included Ronnie. "It makes me too sad," Casey admitted. "And now he's there too. I just can't stand it."

Mikey knew you couldn't expect someone as special as Shawn Macavity even to notice you, if you were as ordinary as Casey Wolsowski. He hadn't even noticed *her*, and she was about the opposite of ordinary, so what did Casey expect?

Mikey was getting ready to give Casey some good advice.

Casey sat drooped over her lunch tray like a daffodil at the end of its life span.

"Don't say it," Margalo warned Mikey.

"What makes you think you know what I'm going to say?" Mikey demanded.

"I don't usually. But this time I do. So don't say it."

"Who died and made you the Queen of me?" Mikey demanded.

"Ha," Margalo said, not even trying to make it sound like a real laugh. She got back to her sandwich, which Mikey was pleased to see looked almost as droopy as Casey.

But Mikey had been reminded. "I have a T-shirt for you. You'll like it. I have almost the exact same one, only not the same color. We can wear them this weekend."

"That'll be exciting," said Margalo. "I'm looking forward to that."

What made her so sarcastic these days? Mikey would have asked, but Casey raised her head to say to Margalo in a totally miserable voice, "They're like in a book, aren't they? Like Romeo and Juliet."

Mikey didn't give Margalo a chance. "What a mean thing to say," she told Casey.

"Why?" Casey wondered, surprised into a little liveliness.

"Because it means they'll be dead soon," Mikey answered. "Unless you plan to gun her down, like Frankie and Johnny. Except she gunned *him* down, didn't she?"

"You don't understand," Casey told her, cross now.

"Yes I do." Mikey had cured Casey of the droops and was pretty pleased with herself.

"But Margalo does," Casey said.

"No she doesn't," Mikey said.

"You think you're so smart, Mikey, but really you're—you're just bossy," Casey announced, surprising all three of them. She picked up her tray and left them alone.

"There's hope for her," Mikey said, while Margalo was telling her, "Good going, Mikey."

"What is making you so sarcastic?" Mikey demanded.

"I'm not. Not about that, I mean, not about Casey."

"You're angry at me, aren't you?" Mikey guessed. "Because of the dance."

"I was," Margalo admitted.

"Angry because you *do* want to go," Mikey guessed.

"Don't you?" Margalo asked. "Secretly, don't you want to go?"

"Not really." But maybe she did. She wasn't exactly sure of herself on this point. And besides, Margalo hadn't said *I told you so*, not once. So Mikey said, "If you want to—I've got a dress, so if you want to we could go. The two of us. If you insist."

"What do you mean, if I insist?"

"Take it or leave it," Mikey said.

"I don't have anything to wear," Margalo said.

"That settles it then. End of topic."

But Mikey wasn't entirely happy about this conclusion, because once she thought about going, she thought that if she went she might get to dance with Shawn. What if the dance she danced with him was a slow dance?

"We've never even been to a party with dancing, with boys," Margalo pointed out. "Probably nobody will dance with us," she told Mikey, as if the going-to-the-dance question was still an open one.

"I thought it's all just everybody dancing with everybody," Mikey said. "Except for slow dances."

"And lots of people stay back during those. There'll be a food table, like last year—"

"Only no Chez ME outside, with *good* food," Mikey reminded her. "But I thought you couldn't go. Because of not having a dress."

"I could find a dress," Margalo said. She announced, as if it was now settled, "You have to come shopping with me."

Mikey didn't feel she had *that* much to make up to Margalo for. "I've got basketball practice. You've got rehearsal. It's not possible." All at once, Mikey really *didn't* want to go to this dance. Because it was one thing to go to school during the day and not have any boy like you or want to go to the dance with you; but if you actually went, nobody there would care at all about your ability to pick up rebounds or serve an ace or even make really good chocolate chip cookies. Everything important for a dance was things Mikey wasn't good at.

"Don't be a total blotch, Mikey," Margalo said. "We'll go

to the Next-to-New Friday. After school. Aurora will take us." Margalo was grinning now, enjoying this. "Or are you going to chicken out?"

"I never chicken out," Mikey said. "Besides, I'll be doing you a favor, since you want to go so badly. Even if you'd never admit it," she concluded, and won that argument.

Then she realized—She was going to the dance.

How had that happened?

# WEEK FOUR

## GIRL GETS ON WITH IT

# 15
# BYE-BYE, LURVE

Margalo's first question to Mikey when she arrived at school on the Monday morning after the dance was the same as her last question before Aurora dropped Mikey off at tennis on Sunday: "Do you want to talk about it?"

Mikey gave the same answer Monday as she had all Saturday night and all Sunday morning: "No." Also, she was wearing her cargoes.

"Have you retired the CK jeans?" Margalo asked.

"No," Mikey said.

So that subject was off-limits too.

But Margalo had confidence. She knew her friend. Sooner or later Mikey would talk, maybe not exactly about how Shawn had ignored Mikey at the dance, or even not exactly about what he'd done to Casey, maybe not exactly about Shawn. But sooner or later, one way or another, Mikey would have an opinion on something about the dance, and the subject would be open.

Margalo knew what she planned to say to Mikey when Mikey did decide to talk. She planned to tell her what Aurora had said: "You can't learn anything if you never make mistakes."

Then Aurora had put it another way. "Making mistakes is how you learn.

"So there are no such things as mistakes," Aurora concluded.

Margalo didn't know about that, and she didn't know about Aurora's logic, but she knew what she'd say to Mikey when the time came. She waited patiently, knowing that with Mikey, there wouldn't be very long to wait.

At their lockers Frannie dashed up to ask, "Isn't it great?"

"You looked like you were having a good time," Margalo answered.

"Not the dance," Frannie said. "The dance was just a dance. I mean Mrs. Brannigan." At their expressions, she explained. "Didn't you hear? Her husband's back."

Mikey had half unzipped her jacket, but she zipped it up again and demanded, "She let him come back? After what he did?"

Frannie nodded, with the kind of smile that happy was named after.

Because she was always looking on the good side of people and events, Frannie Arenberg sometimes missed the obvious,

210

so Margalo pointed it out. "He ran off with another woman and she still wants to be married to him?"

"If my father took my mother back, I'd think he was nuts," Mikey said. "If my mother asked him to, I'd know *she* was."

"People are different," Frannie said.

"How do you know this is true?" Margalo asked. The way rumors grew and spread in junior high, it was like they practiced several different forms of propagation all at the same time—roots spreading underground to pop up as plants in new places, seeds dropped on the soil accidentally by birds or animals, spores blown by the wind or sometimes moved to where they were needed by nature's plan. Rumors had a life cycle of their own. You couldn't always believe what you heard, Margalo knew. "Who told you?" she asked.

Frannie cited her source. "Doucelle's mother went to a workshop—you know how teachers have to keep on getting credits to keep their certification?"

"Why would I know that?" Mikey demanded. "Don't they already have enough to do teaching?"

Frannie ignored this chance to be sidetracked by one of Mikey's R&Rs. "It was a workshop on the self-esteem component of adolescent psychology, and Mrs. Brannigan was there too, but her husband was picking her up at the end. They were going out to dinner."

"Her ex-husband," Margalo said. "Isn't he?"

"I'm not sure about that. But Doucelle told me yesterday after church they're back together."

"I thought you went to Quaker meeting," Mikey objected.

"After *she* got back from church," Frannie specified patiently. "Isn't it great news?" she asked again.

Neither Mikey nor Margalo were willing to commit to that opinion, so Frannie moved on to find a more sympathetic and enthusiastic audience.

"The really good thing about this is, it'll distract people from the dance," Margalo said.

"I told you, I don't want to talk about it," Mikey answered.

That, Margalo ignored. "Unless anything interesting happened that I missed."

"You missed almost everything," Mikey reminded her. "All you did was hide out with the chaperones."

Margalo smiled mysteriously and—she hoped—irritatingly, as if she knew things Mikey couldn't even suspect. Which she did. She smiled and took the conversational offensive. "I thought you didn't want to—"

"I don't."

Mikey turned her back to Margalo and opened her locker. She made the book and paper transfers that would get her through the first two periods. Then she took off her jacket and stuffed it into the locker, keeping her back to Margalo, as if she was hiding something.

Margalo noticed this—how could she not? She also noticed that Mikey was wearing a nonbaggy white T-shirt. The T-shirt actually fitted sort of close to Mikey's back—not tight, but close—and actually looked sort of good with the loose-fitting cargoes. Then Mikey turned around and Margalo saw what was written on the front: I ♥ ME.

Margalo didn't know what to think.

She didn't even know what to say.

It was so—so bold, so outrageous, so blatant—and so sludging stupid. It was just like Mikey to wear a T-shirt that said I ♥ ME. Just exactly like her, and Margalo had to laugh. "That'll get you an A in self-esteem," she said.

Tanisha Harris, passing by, had something to say too: "You tell 'em," she said.

Heather McGinty had a question: "What is *wrong* with her?" she asked her friends as they swept popularly and importantly by.

Ronnie Caselli addressed Mikey directly: "It's not too smart to wear that shirt." Ronnie looked even prettier than usual, so probably she was totally happy being in lurve with Shawn, never mind how he'd acted toward some other people at the dance. Ronnie started to explain, to help Mikey understand. "People might think—"

"I doubt it," Mikey said.

Ronnie, generous in her romantic victory over practically every other girl in the school, was determined to be kind. She warned Mikey, "People will think you're self-centered. Stuck up."

Mikey answered with a *Who-cares?* smile.

"It's your funeral." Her good intentions rejected, Ronnie moved on.

Mikey turned to Margalo. "I got you one too."

Margalo played for time. "You mean a shirt? Really? You got me a present? A shirt like that one?"

"Except yours is black. With white letters, and . . . and originally I got it for Shawn. I'm not talking about him," she reminded Margalo.

"OK," Margalo said, perfectly agreeable. "OK to the shirt, too, but I'm not wearing it to school."

"That's up to you," Mikey said. "It's a free country. If you're chicken."

"Blotch," Margalo said. "But that's good style, with the contrast."

"It's not a style," Mikey answered. "It's what I wanted to wear."

They went on to homeroom, where between Mikey's shirt and Mrs. Brannigan's husband, people didn't have much time to debate whether Louis and Sal Caselli had really—as they claimed—brought a six-pack to the dance and hidden it in the tank of one of the toilets in the boys' bathroom. "Didn't want to lose the chill, dude." They didn't have time to wonder what it meant that Ralph had brought Heather Thomas to the dance but never—not once—danced a slow dance with her. "Although, neither one of them danced slow with anyone else." Nobody had time to replay the big drama of the evening either, more than to ask one another, "Is that Casey girl in school today?" or "Did anyone talk to Casey yesterday? Margalo, did you?"

"Why me?" Mikey demanded.

She shoveled the chicken-and-rice casserole into her mouth as quickly as she could because there were four girls standing there telling her she had to, so she was probably going to have her lunch cut short. But she kept on trying to get out of it. "Why not Margalo? She's actually a friend of Casey's, aren't you, Margalo?"

"It has to be you because you're in the same boat with her," a girl named Alice told Mikey. Alice, who had fine, straight carroty red hair and big glasses, was Casey's best friend. They had spent seventh grade together on the outskirts of the preppy clique. But this group standing in front of Mikey and Margalo's cafeteria table had Annaliese in it too, and Derrie, and even Aimi, from Margalo's play. This was a mixed group.

"Same boat because of Shawn," Aimi explained.

"I don't want to talk about him," Mikey said.

"Neither do we," they said.

"So, will you?" Alice asked. "Because she can't just stay home from school for the rest of her life, and she wouldn't talk to me."

"What makes you think she'll talk to me?" Mikey demanded, still eating away. Actually, she liked being asked. Ordinarily they'd have chosen Margalo, but today, of the two, they chose Mikey.

"Couldn't you just try?" Alice asked. "She was really upset. At the dance."

"I was there," Mikey reminded them.

"Her mother's really upset too," Alice added.

"I don't want to hear any more about it," Mikey said.

"I don't think she's eaten anything since Saturday," Alice said.

"All *right*," Mikey said to call a halt to this list of pitiful-nesses.

"And I'm really worried," Alice said. "Really, really worried," she said, looking at Mikey out of pale blue eyes, like a desperate rabbit. "What if she does something . . . to herself?" she asked, unable to say this above a whisper, unable to give it its real name.

Luckily Margalo spoke up. "I'll do it if you won't," she told Mikey. "But you'd be better."

"I *said* I would, didn't I?" Mikey demanded. "I said all right. I'll call her."

"When?" Alice asked. She might be rabbity, but she was also persistent.

"Tonight?" Derrie suggested.

"Now," Mikey decided. She stood up, abandoning her half-eaten lunch. "Why wait?"

On her way out of the cafeteria she passed the table where Ronnie and Shawn sat at the center. They looked like a couple in a movie, in one of the scenes that show the audience how much they're in love—eating together; quick cut to walking and talking together, always in good weather; quick cut to shopping for CDs, sharing the earphones, always having a wonderful, wonderful time. Mikey had expected to feel some twinges—jealousy, heart-ache (but not -break; it would take more than Shawn Macavity to break *her* heart), maybe a little leftover longing—but she could barely remember what all the Shawn Macavity feelings had felt like. "Hunh," she grunted at them, passing by, and maybe they looked up at her, maybe they didn't.

*Muck and mire*, she thought. Feelings that were so strong shouldn't just end, just be over, just like that. Should they? Was that at all normal for lurve? She wanted to ask someone, but Margalo didn't know anything about it.

It was early enough in the second lunch period for both pay phones to be available. Alice, who had followed her, knew Casey's number by heart, and Derrie, who had also followed, had a quarter. That made three girls trailing close behind her, although Margalo barely counted. Mikey ignored them all and punched the numbers Alice told her into the keypad. Punch-punch-punch, punch-punch, punch-punch. It barely rang before a woman picked it up, asking, "Dr. Thomaston?"

"No, it's Mikey Elsinger," Mikey said. "Is Casey there?"

"Who?" the woman asked.

"Mikey. From school. Can I talk to her?"

"I've never heard of you," the woman said, puzzled.

"Yes, you have," Mikey told her patiently. "I play tennis. And basketball. I make cookies." She thought. "I'm Margalo's friend."

"Oh, you're that one," the woman said.

Mikey waited, but the woman just waited right back at her, so Mikey asked again, "Can I talk to Casey?" Either Casey had the driftiest mother in all of West Junior High, or this woman was seriously worrying about her daughter.

"But not for long. I'm expecting a call."

"I know," Mikey said.

"How do you know?" the woman asked.

Poor Casey, if this dimwit was her mother. Or maybe lucky Casey, to matter so much.

"*Is* Casey there?" Mikey asked. It was important, in tennis and in conversation, to keep focused. "Can I talk to her?"

"I'll see. I guess. Wait here."

Mikey looked at Margalo and rolled her eyes.

"What's she saying?" Alice asked, and Mikey shook her head, *Not now, don't interrupt.*

Then Casey was on the phone. "Mikey?" she asked, her voice thick with tears, unless she had developed a really bad cold on Sunday. But her voice was also a little curious.

"Why aren't you in school?" Mikey demanded.

"You went to school today?" Now Casey sounded as if Mikey had just discovered the cure for cancer.

"Why shouldn't I? He didn't—" Margalo punched her on the arm, and Mikey got it. She shut up. Then she started again. "Face it, Casey, you have to come back sometime, and I can promise you, it'll be worse tomorrow."

"It couldn't," Casey said, her voice now little, whispery. "I can't."

"Why not?"

"It's . . . I'm . . . You know why."

"Tell your mother to bring you in before lunch is over," Mikey instructed.

"No." Casey's voice started thickening again. "I really can't, I—"

"Then I'll get *my* mother to pick me up, and I'll come get you."

"Your mother lives in the city," Casey reminded her sadly.

"So what? She's got a car."

"She's got a job." Casey was getting impatient.

"So what?"

"*And* she got married last week and moved to L.A." Casey announced.

"Dallas," Mikey corrected. "So, so what? I'll get Margalo's mother to—"

"You are so *bossy*," Casey said. "I give up."

"Good," Mikey said, and slammed the phone back onto its cradle.

She looked at Margalo and warned her, "I've done it. Now I'm going to eat my dessert."

When they were seated again, Mikey told Margalo her not-so-personal news. "He called again."

"Not Shawn," Margalo guessed. "Your Secret Admirer," she guessed.

"You probably already know who it is."

Margalo shook her head and took out a waxed-paper-wrapped

package of homemade peanut butter crackers.

"Neither do I," Mikey said. "He has some good ideas, though. About . . . I'll tell you about them—how we could make Chez ME a real business. I asked him how he liked your outfit for the dance, but he didn't know what it was."

"He could have been pretending not to know," Margalo suggested.

Neither one of them considered the unlikely possibility that anybody at the dance wouldn't have noticed the one girl in pants, long silk pants and a long-sleeved, flowing white shirt, easily the most elegant female there. They both knew that if there had been an Outfit Prize awarded, Margalo would have won it.

"But what was the point of getting so dressed up if all you were going to do was talk to teachers?" Mikey asked, telling Margalo, "You should have come into the bathroom with me for the slow dances." Then she got back to what interested her. "I told him about you not asking me to be stage manager. He asked me why I didn't apply to be an assistant stage manager, if I wanted to be involved. I told him, I don't want to be anybody's assistant, and he guessed that decided it. But do you think I could?"

"Why would you want to work on the play now? I thought—you *are* through with Shawn, aren't you?"

"I don't want to talk about him." But how did Margalo know? Mikey wondered, and once she wondered, she couldn't not ask. "How'd you know that?"

"The way you look," Margalo said. She shrugged. "What you're talking about. Who you look at. It's like, you're really *here*. Talking to me. You're back to being really you, not—the way you were trying to get his attention, buying his favor with cookies—"

"OK. I get it. You can stop now."

"So I think you're over him," Margalo concluded.

"I'm sort of embarrassed," Mikey admitted. "But I'm not sorry."

"I know what you mean," Margalo said.

Mikey believed her, but how *did* Margalo know? She was about to ask, but Margalo changed the subject.

"Want to stop by and congratulate the happy couple?" she asked Mikey.

Sometimes Margalo was just—dense. "Why would I want to do something like that?"

Margalo just smiled.

After a minute Mikey saw the possibilities.

"Abso-grime-ing-lutely," she said. She should have known better. Margalo was never dense.

They got up, Mikey carrying her tray and Margalo a brown paper bag filled with crumpled pieces of waxed paper. They crossed the cafeteria together and stopped together at the table where Ronnie and Shawn now sat alone. Alone and holding hands; and holding hands on top of the table, for everybody to see and envy them.

"Hey, Mikey," Ronnie said.

Shawn didn't say anything.

Ronnie said, "Hey, Margalo."

Mikey got the first word. "Shawn," she said. "You know what you said about being friends?"

He looked at Ronnie, raised his eyebrows—*Didn't I tell you?*—looked back at Mikey. "Yeah?"

"I should tell you, I'm not interested," Mikey said. "I'm pretty fussy about who my friends are."

He considered this unexpected development. "Izzat why you're wearing my shirt?"

Mikey smiled, a *How-dumb-can-you-be?* smile. "It's not your shirt," she told him. "It's mine."

She was ready to go, but Margalo had her own ideas.

"You know, Ronnie," Margalo said, "you're a really good liar." Margalo's voice was the same one she would have used to tell Ronnie she had great hair or a great body, two indisputably true and obvious things.

Ronnie was trying to figure out whether to swell up with preening or to get angry with insult.

"Probably it's because you've had so many boyfriends to practice on. Do you think?" Margalo asked, as cool as if she was in seminar, thinking about why the ancient Egyptians might have believed that the sky was a cow. "I mean, before this one," Margalo explained. "Everybody says how good you are at getting a new boyfriend whenever you want. Everybody's really glad Shawn gets to have a turn."

Ronnie smiled a tack-sitting smile and extracted her hand

from Shawn's. "Hey," he protested, "what's wrong with you?"

Mikey and Margalo left the cafeteria and went out into the hall, and were almost back to their lockers before Margalo announced, "We were good." And Mikey echoed her, "We were bad."

Because Frannie had forewarned them, Margalo saw immediately the differences in Mrs. Brannigan. It wasn't just the dyed hair or the deep smoky blue turtlenecked sweater over gray flannel slacks—although these made a difference, as did the light makeup the teacher was wearing these days. The real difference was the goofy, lit-from-within look on Mrs. Brannigan's face.

But the teacher wasn't any less sharp, Margalo was relieved to notice; Mrs. Brannigan was still teaching full steam. Margalo looked at Frannie across the long table and nodded her head.

Frannie smiled back, a big, toothy grin. The thing about Frannie that took such getting used to was that she really was nice. Frannie was a mystery to Margalo, which was one of the reasons Margalo enjoyed having her around. Why, for example, should it make Frannie so happy for some teacher to get her husband back?

After class, as they gathered up books to go on to earth science, Mikey asked Margalo and Frannie, "Why would she take him back after he ran off with that gym teacher?"

Frannie had the answer. "They're married." But she had

223

something else she wanted to talk to them about. "My mother got her next job."

"You're moving," Margalo realized, and then, "Does that mean you won't be in the play?"

"Mom's going next month, but the rest of us are staying through the end of the school year. Then we'll join her in Hawaii."

"Hawaii?" Mikey said. "I've never been there."

"But I'm going to have a big party before," Frannie said.

"I've never been farther west than California," Mikey said.

"It'll be in May, a going-away party," Frannie said. "So I want you to think about if you'll come to it."

Mikey was suspicious. "Like a dance?"

"There'll be dancing," Frannie said. "And boys," she added unnecessarily.

Margalo figured that she knew what Frannie was thinking, telling them this early; and she knew it meant Frannie really wanted them to come to this party of hers.

Frannie said, "I don't know if you're—are you ready for boys?"

"Hunh," Mikey snorted. "Are *they* ready for *us*?"

Mikey wanted to know, so she asked. Frannie and Margalo went off to science, but Mikey went up to Mrs. Brannigan. "Mrs. Brannigan? If your husband is back—"

"Yes?" the teacher asked. She was waiting for her next seminar group. She had her books spread out on the table in

front of her—the art book, the mythology book, the Bible—
and she had drawn maps of Renaissance cities on the board
behind her, arrows marking the routes the armies of the con-
dottieri had traveled. Mikey stood right next to the teacher,
and Mrs. Brannigan looked up at her. "Mikey, yes. He is," she
said, and sounded glad.

"Why did you let him?" Mikey asked.

"What?" Mrs. Brannigan asked. "You mean, let him come
back?"

"Yeah," Mikey said.

The teacher looked at the clock and she looked back at
Mikey. Her face got pink, but she decided to answer. "Short
and simple: I wanted to."

Mikey nodded. That made sense.

"But," Mrs. Brannigan said, "I wouldn't a second time,
Mikey."

Mikey nodded again. "Only two chances."

Like all the other teachers, Mrs. Brannigan had been at the
dance as a chaperone. She'd been there and seen how things
went. "More like, two strikes and you're out," she said.

Mikey had to let her have the last word, because if she didn't
run, she was going to be late to science, and Mr. Schramm
made you stay as many minutes late after class as you had
arrived, which made you late for your next class too, and who
needed the accumulating aggravation?

Besides, she didn't have anything better than that to say.

# 16
# THE COUNTRY
# OF THE BLIND

Tuesday's rehearsal went more smoothly, now that the dance was over and done with, on its way to being mostly forgotten and maybe not all that important after all. Now the play was the thing. Ms. Larch started out with Shawn, who seemed at least to be trying. Margalo happened to know that Ms. Larch had given the actor an ultimatum: Learn lines, or else. And Ms. Larch didn't need to specify what she meant by *or else*. Margalo started out with Ira and Jason, who were much more prepared than Shawn was, and more attentive, except that Ira was always looking over to where Heather Thomas and Rhonda rehearsed together. Heather, Margalo noticed, was always looking back.

Which probably explained why Heather and Ralph had broken up. But Margalo would never have thought of Ira as a person who would steal someone else's girlfriend.

Although, the person who got stolen had something to do with it too, didn't she?

Halfway through the after-school activities period, Ms. Larch called Heather and Rhonda over to hear them speak their lines, and Margalo got Shawn and Frannie for their Act I scene. Margalo hadn't realized how much time and work it took just to get this first step accomplished; even after two and a half weeks of rehearsals they were nowhere near finished with memorizing. She set her desk to face Frannie's and Shawn's desks and asked Melissa to join them. Melissa, she knew, had learned all her first-act lines, and Frannie knew hers; that would put the pressure on Shawn.

As they got into it Shawn stood up and moved around a little, which seemed to help him remember. "You're making fun of Margaret in that line," Margalo advised him. "Thomas makes fun of everybody. Including himself."

Shawn looked down at them as he considered that. "I guess that makes sense, if he's so sick of people. Do you think that makes sense, Frannie?"

Frannie nodded agreement but didn't say anything or look at him. She had been, Margalo thought, immune to Shawn, like there are people who are immune to poison ivy. Melissa spoke her lines, and then it was Frannie again, but when she came to the part about how attractive she found a well-dressed man, and how when she was young, she had often lost her heart to a clean shirt drying on a hedge, without a man inside it, Margalo saw the way Frannie's brown spaniel eyes rested on Shawn's blue work shirt. Seeing, she realized Frannie wasn't one bit immune.

Margalo was shocked.

At the end of rehearsal Louis Caselli came strutting up to their little group. He spoke to Frannie first, to tell her, "I can't have any girlfriend in Hawaii. Sorry, but—what good would that do me?"

"None," she agreed.

"Like I said," he agreed. That settled, he turned to Shawn to ask, "Now that you and Ronnie are together, we're practically cousins. You and me, I mean, because me and Ronnie already are—we've been cousins all my life. So you should let me in on some of the stuff you do that gets you chicks. I mean, man, you dump all over them and they just come back for more. You're *amazing*. I figure, you could be a big help to me, now Frannie's moving to Hawaii. You gotta know something. You know?"

"Well," Shawn said. "I could try."

Louis punched him on the shoulder to express his pleasure and excitement and confidence. The others went off, leaving Margalo and Frannie together.

Margalo asked Frannie, "Did you talk to Casey when she came in yesterday?" Frannie nodded. "What excuse did she give?"

"A dentist appointment," Frannie said. "She had *Lord of the Rings*, and she was reading it."

"I don't blame her," Margalo said.

The two looked over to where Shawn and Rhonda were having a little flirt fest.

"Neither do I," Frannie said. "I blame him. But I never thought he was anything special, not as a person. The only special thing about him is his looks. Although, his *looks* . . ." Frannie knew she didn't have to finish the sentence. "I'll be sort of glad to get away from them," she told Margalo.

Ronnie came to wait in the classroom doorway. Basketball practice was over and she was there to join up with her boyfriend, but she wasn't going to come into the room to claim him. She was accustomed to having boys coming up to claim *her*.

Shawn stayed right where he was, waiting for Ronnie to come to him.

"I console myself with remembering how many movie stars looked like dorks in high school," Margalo told Frannie, "and thinking of how that could work the other way around, too."

Ronnie stayed waiting where she was, and Shawn stayed waiting where he was. Margalo and Frannie stayed where they were and watched.

"I'm going to miss you," Frannie said.

As they watched, Mikey came to the doorway and walked right through the line of sight connecting Ronnie and Shawn as if it wasn't there—as if, even if it was there, it was something in another dimension that had nothing to do with her and was of no interest to her. Mikey just strode on through, practically tripping over Hadrian Klenk who tried to ask her something, ignoring everything except what she had in mind.

"And Mikey, too," Frannie said. Mikey came up and Frannie said, "It won't be the same without you, next year in Hawaii."

"You could invite us to come live with you," Mikey suggested, then reassured Frannie, "That was a joke." She turned to Margalo. "You didn't ask Ms. Larch about the stage manager having an assistant, did you? Because I changed my mind. I don't have the time, I've got tennis and Chez ME. Did you ask her?"

"Not yet."

"And *you* don't have the time either," Mikey warned Margalo. "Now what's so funny?" she demanded of Frannie.

Frannie didn't answer. Instead she said, "I like your T-shirt."

"If Margalo doesn't want it, you can have hers," Mikey offered.

"Who said I don't want it?" Margalo protested. "That stinks, giving Frannie something you already gave me, Mikey."

"I said *if*," Mikey argued.

"And right in front of me," Margalo pointed out.

"I really am going to miss you two," Frannie said, laughing.

They jounced along side by side on the leather seat of the late bus. Margalo turned away from the window to tell Mikey—

as the bus lurched to a stop and they surged forward in unison like synchronized swimmers—"I'm giving Shawn and Ronnie three weeks."

Mikey had a more immediate concern. "You'd think that they'd put seat belts on school buses. Wouldn't you?"

"Write to the President," Margalo said, as if she'd heard all this before.

"Maybe I will," Mikey said, although she knew she wouldn't. Margalo *had* heard all this before, she realized, and there were other things Margalo had been wanting to talk about all day, and all yesterday, too, and Sunday. Mikey decided it was time to put Margalo out of her misery. She was ready to do that now. She admitted, "I was wrong about Shawn."

Margalo didn't try to contradict her. "Everybody makes mistakes," she said irritatingly.

"I don't," Mikey said. "Other people might say I do, but usually I don't agree with them."

"This time almost everybody agreed with *you*," Margalo pointed out.

"And as usual they were wrong. I was just wrong right along with them for once."

"Mistakes are how you learn," Margalo said, which sounded to Mikey like Aurora's lopsided way of looking at things, a little wacko and usually worth thinking about—later. Now she had more interesting things on her mind.

"I'm looking forward to the next time I fall in lurve," she told Margalo. "It's pretty much fun."

This, Margalo paid close attention to. "You think so?"

"Only next time I'm choosing someone entirely different."

"You don't *choose* who you fall in love with," Margalo told her.

Mikey was about to say, Who appointed you Love Information Center? Then she had a guess, an intuitive leap, and she knew, she just all at once *knew*—

"*I* plan to choose," Mikey argued while the back of her mind chased after this new idea she was having. Speaking from the front of her mind, she told Margalo, "I'm thinking of Ralph now that he and Heather are through."

She *knew*, and she knew she was right, too.

Margalo was in lurve. And had been, all along, hadn't she? But not with Shawn Macavity; this had started long before Shawn. But Margalo had been so secret and quiet about it, kept it so private to herself—it was impressive how Margalo had kept it to herself. Mikey was impressed. She really admired Margalo sometimes; sometimes she just *really* admired her friend.

"Although, you choose what you *do* about it," Margalo said.

"He's going to be my mixed doubles partner," Mikey explained.

"So I guess you could choose *not* to be in love."

"So we'll have lots in common."

Mikey decided right then she wasn't going to tell Margalo that she had figured it out. If Margalo wanted it to be a secret,

Mikey wouldn't say one thing. She even had a guess about who, but she wasn't going to tell Margalo that, either. Or her opinion of him. Besides, Margalo already knew what a non-event of a teacher she thought he was.

"So maybe," Margalo argued, arguing herself around to what Mikey had just said, "you really *do* choose."

"I think I *should* try for Ralph," Mikey decided.

Margalo said, sarcastic, "Lucky Ralph. Although, you know what they say: Love is blind."

"No it isn't," Mikey said.

"OK, it's half-blind," Margalo said. "Blind to faults."

"People are what's blind," Mikey said.

"Which means that the blinder love is, the better for all of us," Margalo said.

Margalo always wanted to have the last word. Maybe this time Mikey would let her.

Margalo, of course, had even more to say. "You know what else they say? In the country of the blind the one-eyed man is King."

Mikey couldn't stand it. "Or Queen," she said.